PR

DON
New York
ron

DARK KINGS SERIES

"A breathtaking tale...I absolutely loved it!"
–Romance Junkies on Dark Craving

"Loaded with subtle emotions, sizzling chemistry and some provocative thoughts on real choices [Grant's] characters are forced to make as they choose their loves for eternity."
- RT Book Reviews on Dark Heat

"Vivid images, intense details and enchanting characters grab the reader's attention and [don't] let go."
–Night Owl Reviews on Dark Heat

DARK WARRIORS SERIES

"Evie and Malcolm is a couple that makes it impossible not to love them."
–The Jeep Diva

"Grant's smoldering seventh Dark Warrior outing will grip readers from the first page, immersing them in her wounded, lonely couple's journey of redemption...each scene is filled with Grant's clever, complex characters and trademark sizzle."
–Romantic Times Magazine (RT Book Reviews)

**Don't miss these other spellbinding novels by
DONNA GRANT**

DARK KING SERIES

Dark Heat
Darkest Flame
Fire Rising

DARK WARRIOR SERIES

Midnight's Master
Midnight's Lover
Midnight's Seduction
Midnight's Warrior
Midnight's Kiss
Midnight's Captive
Midnight's Temptation
Midnight's Promise
Midnight's Surrender

DARK SWORD SERIES

Dangerous Highlander
Forbidden Highlander
Wicked Highlander
Untamed Highlander
Shadow Highlander
Darkest Highlander

CHIASSON SERIES

Wild Fever

SHIELD SERIES

A Dark Guardian
A Kind of Magic
A Dark Seduction
A Forbidden Temptation
A Warrior's Heart

DRUIDS GLEN SERIES

Highland Mist
Highland Nights
Highland Dawn
Highland Fires
Highland Magic
Dragonfyre

SISTERS OF MAGIC TRILOGY

Shadow Magic
Echoes of Magic
Dangerous Magic

Royal Chronicles Novella Series

Prince of Desire
Prince of Seduction
Prince of Love
Prince of Passion

Wicked Treasures Novella Series

Seized by Passion
Enticed by Ecstasy
Captured by Desire

Stand Alone Stories

Savage Moon (ebook novella)
Forever Mine (ebook novella)
Mutual Desire

**And look for more anticipated novels
from Donna Grant**

Darkest Flame (Dark Kings)
Wild Dream – (Chiasson)
Fire Rising – (Dark Kings)

coming soon!

THE CRAVING

ROGUES OF SCOTLAND

DONNA GRANT

THE CRAVING

© 2014 by DL Grant, LLC
Excerpt from *Darkest Flame* copyright © 2014 by Donna Grant

Cover design © 2014 by Leah Suttle

ISBN 10: 0991454219
ISBN 13: 978-0991454211

www.DonnaGrant.com

Available in ebook and print editions

ACKNOWLEDGEMENTS

A special thanks goes out to my wonderful team that helps me get these books out – Melissa Bradley, Stephanie Dalvit, and Leah Suttle. You guys are the bomb. Seriously. Hats off to my editor, Chelle Olsen, and cover design extraordinaire, Leah Suttle. Thank you all for helping me to keep my crazy schedule and keeping me sane!

There's no way I could do any of this without my amazing family – Steve, Gillian, and Connor – thanks for putting up with my hectic schedule and for knowing when it was time that I got out of the house for a spell. And special nod to the Grant pets – Lexi, Sheba, Sassy, Tinkerbell, and Diego – who love to walk on the keyboard or demand some loving regardless of what I'm doing.

Last but not least, my readers. You have my eternal gratitude for the amazing support you show me and my books. Y'all rock my world. Stay tuned at the end of this story for a sneak peek of *Darkest Flame*, Dark Kings book 1 out April 29, 2014. Enjoy!

xoxo
Donna

PROLOGUE

Highlands of Scotland
Summer, 1427

Ronan Galt brought his mount to a halt at the top of the mountain, his gaze taking in the majestic view of the wild Highlands. His gaze lowered to the valley below, and a smile broke over his face when he spotted his three friends in the valley.

A small nudge from his knee, and his horse was racing down the mountain, deftly missing the rocks protruding from the ground.

"About time," Stefan grumbled crossly once Ronan reached them.

Ronan raised his brow as he looked into Stefan's hazel gaze. "You might want to reign in that tempter, my friend. We're going to be around beautiful women this night. Women require smiles and sweet words. No' furrowed brows."

There was laughter from everyone but Stefan, who gave Ronan a droll look.

"Aye, we've heard enough about this Ana," Daman said as he turned his mount alongside Ronan's. "Take me to this gypsy beauty so I can see her for myself."

Ronan regarded his friend sternly. "You think to take her from me?"

Daman's confident smile grew as his eyes twinkled in merriment. "Is she that beautiful?"

"Just you try," Ronan dared Daman, only half jesting.

Morcant shoved his long, sandy blond hair out of his eyes with his hand. "Be cautious, Ronan. You wrong a gypsy, and they'll curse you. No' so sure we should be meddling with such people."

Ronan laughed and reined in his jittery mount. "Ah, but with such a willing body, how am I to refuse Ana? Come, my friends, and let us enjoy the bounty that awaits."

He gave a short whistle and his horse surged forward in a run. Ronan didn't wait for his three comrades, because he knew they would follow – no matter what.

It began a decade earlier when they chanced upon one another during the Highland games between their four clans. After that, they made sure to meet regularly until they were as inseparable as brothers. The four formed a friendship that grew tighter with each year that passed.

Ronan looked over his shoulder to find the

other three racing each other trying to catch him. He spurred his stallion faster, the wind brushing his face, and the ground a blur beneath his horse's hooves.

One by one, the three caught him. Ronan pulled up, easing his stallion into a canter until they rode their horses four abreast. A glance showed that even Stefan's face had eased into something that could almost be considered a smile.

Ronan grunted when he spotted two riders atop a hill. Even from the distance he recognized the plaid of his clan. It came as no surprise that his laird would have him watched. He was, after all, Ronan's uncle.

He and his friends rode from one glen to another until Ronan finally slowed his horse to a walk. With his friends beside him, they stopped atop the next hill and looked down at the circle of gypsy wagons hidden in the wooded glen below.

"I've a bad feeling," Daman said as he shifted uncomfortably atop his mount. "We shouldna be here."

Morcant's horse flung up his head, but he easily brought his mount under control with soft words. "I've a need to sink my rod betwixt willing thighs. If you doona wish to partake, Daman, then doona, but you willna be stopping me."

"Nor me," Ronan said. Normally he would have listened to Daman, but he had been to the gypsy camp for four days straight and left without any difficulties.

Stefan was silent for several moments before he

gave Ronan a nod of agreement.

Ronan was the first to ride down the hill to the camp. A young beauty with long black hair came running out to greet him in her brightly colored skirts. He pulled his horse to a halt and jumped off with a smile as Ana launched herself into his arms.

He caught her and brought his lips down to hers. Ah, but she had the most alluring lips. They could bring him to the point of ecstasy.

"I've missed you," she said in her thick Romanian accent.

"Is that so?" he asked with a wink. He turned her to the others who had ridden up behind him. "Ana, these are my friends, Daman, Morcant, and Stefan," he said, pointing to each of them in turn.

Her smile was wide as she held out her arm. "Welcome to our camp."

Morcant was the first to dismount. He dropped the reins to allow his horse to graze and walked between two wagons into the center of the camp.

It didn't take Stefan long to follow. Ronan saw the indecision on Daman's face. It was long moments until Daman slid from his horse and gathered the reins of all four mounts to tether them together.

"I'll keep watch," Daman said as he sat outside the camp near a tree.

Ronan wrapped an arm around Ana, briefly wondering why Daman was suddenly wary of the gypsies. Then Ana rubbed her bountiful breasts against him, and Ronan forgot everything but his aching cock.

He didn't give any of his friends a second thought as Ana took him to her wagon. Ronan wasted no time in quickly undressing her. His body was starved, and the gypsy was an enthusiastic and willing accomplice.

~ ~ ~

Ronan yawned, his body fully sated after hours in Ana's arms. Damn, but the little gypsy knew how to wring pleasure from him. He was lucky to have found her. He closed his eyes and was lulled by the haunting melody of the violins being played around the camp's fire.

He was drifting off to sleep when Ana snuggled against him, one leg thrown over his. She was tenacious about lying against him.

"When will we marry?" she asked.

His drowsy mind was yanked from the fringes of sleep. "Hmm?" Surely he hadn't heard her mention marriage. Theirs was just a mutual meeting of pleasure.

He'd made sure to give her multiple orgasms. Wasn't that enough? Marriage – or any long-term commitment – had never been uttered. He knew that for a fact.

"Marriage, Ronan," she said, rolling the R in his name.

Now he was wide awake, a vise around his chest. His heart thumped, his blood pounded in his ears. Marriage was a word he never wanted associated with him, much less mentioned. It was something he intended never to partake in.

Ever.

He pretended to be asleep hoping Ana would drop the matter. It took great effort for him to remain where he was, and not jump up and ride far, far away.

All he had to do was convince her marriage was a bad idea. Then he would wait until she slept and leave. Never to return.

Perhaps he should have listened to Daman and not visited Ana this night.

She nudged him with a slight laugh. "Wake up, Ronan. You've come to see me for five nights now. You've shared my bed. You've eaten the food I've cooked. It's time to speak with my family about what you plan to do."

Do? What he planned to do was get up and leave. Aye. Fast. How had he gotten into this mess? He thought he'd be safe from any mention of the word marriage by dallying with the gypsies. Apparently he'd been wrong.

"Ronan," she said louder.

He cracked open an eye, feigning sleep. "Aye?"

"Will we leave in the morning to meet your family?"

"Nay, sweet Ana," he said and closed his eyes with a fake yawn. She had given him such enjoyment the last few days, he would let her down gently, and then pleasure her again before he left. Maybe a lie would be best. Yes, a lie. Something where he didn't have to explain his family or his past – or his abhorrence to marriage.

"I'm promised to another."

The bed moved as she flopped on her back and then sat up. Had he gotten out of the marriage business with just that small lie? Ronan sure hoped so.

He heard her moving about the small wagon. A brief look showed she was gathering her clothes. He'd remain until she was out of the wagon, and then he would sneak out. At least that was his plan until she sank onto the edge of the narrow bed after dressing and began to cry.

How he hated when women used tears. His mother and sister did it often enough, and he was immune to such machinations because of it. His desire for Ana waned to nothing and then quickly turned to revulsion.

Once more a female had tried to use him.

She had succeeded in snaring him with her body, but not marriage. When that hadn't worked, she resorted to tears as they all did.

"I love you, Ronan," Ana murmured.

He squeezed his eyes shut. A part of him, a cruel, vicious part, wanted to tell her that there was no such thing as love. Love was a tool used by women to entrap men. His father had fallen into such a trap, as had his brother-in-law.

Ronan had tried to tell his brother-in-law, but the besotted fool had actually thought Ronan's sister loved him. What she loved was the money her husband had.

A memory from when Ronan was just a lad filled his mind. He witnessed a fight between his parents where his father vowed his love, and his mother laughed in his face. Then and there Ronan knew that love was just a word. There was no meaning, no emotion that poets wrote about or minstrels sang about.

He blew out a harsh breath and rose from the bed as he grabbed his kilt. "I think it's time I left."

"No marriage?" Ana asked, tears pouring heedlessly down her face.

Ronan gave a quick jerk of his head side to side and fastened his kilt. Ana cried even harder as she rushed from the wagon. He let out a deep breath and pulled on his boots. After his sword was belted into place he found his saffron shirt.

Just as he was reaching for it he heard an anguished scream, a soul-deep, fathomless cry that was drug from the depths of someone's soul.

Ronan forgot about the shirt as he leapt from the wagon, his hand on the hilt of his sword, ready to battle whatever had disrupted the camp.

He looked one way and then the other for the threat, but found only Daman standing outside the wagons. He was staring past Ronan with a resigned expression on his face. Ronan turned and found the old woman, Ilinca, who was often with Ana, looking down at something in the grass.

Ronan took a step toward her and instantly came to a halt when he spotted Ana's bright pink and blue skirts. Even in the fading light of evening there was no mistaking the dark stain upon the grass as anything but blood.

"What the hell," Morcant said as he exited a

wagon still fastening his kilt.

The night of pleasure and laughter Ronan had envisioned with his friends seemed as far away as the stars in the sky. He wanted to go to Ana, but with the dagger sticking out of her stomach – and her hand still around it – the last place he needed to be was the gypsy camp.

They would blame her suicide on him, all because he refused to take her as his wife.

"Ronan," Stefan called urgently as he stood amid a group of gypsies.

There would be no walking away. If Ronan wanted to leave with his life, he and his friends were going to have to fight their way through the group of gypsies who stood with various weapons.

Before he could pull out his sword, Ilinca let loose a shriek and pointed her gnarled finger at him. Ronan was frozen, unable to move or even speak.

Words tumbled from Ilinca's mouth, her wrinkled face a mask of grief and fury. He may not comprehend the words, but he knew they could be nothing good. Especially since she was somehow holding him immobile.

Morcant, however, wasn't in such a bind. He rushed to Ilinca with his sword raised, but in a heartbeat, the old woman had him frozen in his tracks as well.

A bellow of anger rose up in Ronan, but he couldn't let it loose. He was only able to shift his eyes. He tried desperately to silently tell Stefan and Daman to run, but he should've known his friends wouldn't leave.

The ever-present rage exploded in Stefan and he let out a battle cry worthy of his clan as he leapt over the fire toward Ilinca. But once more, the old gypsy used her magic to halt him.

Her gaze shifted, and Ronan found his own on Daman. Daman glanced at the ground and inhaled deeply. Then, with purposeful strides, crossed some unseen barrier into the camp.

Instantly, Ronan's head exploded with pain. He squeezed his eyes shut, but there was no blocking it out. It seemed to go on for eternity.

As quickly as it came, it was gone. When he opened his eyes, there was nothing but blackness. There was no sound, no movement.

"This is for my Ana," Ilinca's disembodied voice in her thick Romanian accent suddenly declared around him. "You killed her as surely as if you held the blade yourself. For that I curse you, Ronan Galt. Forever will you be locked in here until such time as you earn your freedom."

Ronan turned one way and then the other. He ran until he couldn't run any more, and then went another direction and ran for miles. And still it was always the same.

Blackness.

Where were Daman, Morcant, and Stefan? How was he supposed to earn his freedom? He hated the stillness, hated the silence. But more than anything, he hated being alone.

CHAPTER ONE

Ravensclyde Castle
Northern Scotland 1609

"Nay!" Meg Alpin screamed as two wolfhounds bounded around her. They knocked her off her feet to land in a tangle of skirts, though they did nothing to cushion her fall. "You great big oafs!"

No amount of scolding could rein in the dogs now that they were inside the room. The white sheets draped over the furniture were only something for them to pull off and play tug-of-war with.

Meg shook her head and climbed to her feet as she dusted herself off. She then put her hands on her hips and rolled her eyes. As if she didn't already have enough on her hands. As mad as she wanted to be at the wolfhounds, she couldn't quite manage it.

She understood what it was to be left behind. The dogs had been all but forgotten until she arrived three months earlier. She had lavished them with affection and attention. In return, they had become the animals they should have been – loyal, protective, clever. And with their antics, they were obviously making up for lost time.

"Enough!" she called and clapped her hands together.

The two wolfhounds immediately dropped the sheet they had been tugging between them and loped over to her. She gave them a rub on their heads and pointed out the door.

"Go chase some rabbits."

With their tongues lolling out of their mouths, the wolfhounds took off at a dead run, skittering around a corner before disappearing – loudly – down the stairs. There was a distant shriek, letting Meg know the dogs had scared one of the maids again.

She was smiling even as she shook her head. The wolfhounds might think she was their savior, but the dogs had helped her as well. Most nights she had one on each side of her in the bed. Somehow, they always knew when she would give in to her tears. They would leave their spots before the fire and jump up on the bed to lay with her, as if protecting her from the memories that wouldn't let go.

Meg squared her shoulders and took a look around the large room, her eyes flitting over each covered piece. Her great-aunt had offered her refuge at Ravensclyde. In doing so, Aunt Tilly had given her leave to rearrange the castle as Meg saw fit.

After nearly a month of sitting and staring off into nothing with a book in her lap, reliving the last half year of her life, she finally realized that if she didn't do something she would waste away to nothing.

Since she needed to occupy her days – and her mind - going through the old furniture that was stored in the top floor of the tower seemed a great place to start.

Meg pulled the first sheet off what turned out to be a large wardrobe and promptly began coughing from all the dust. She waved away the particles she could see in the sunlight that filtered through the windows.

She turned her head before pulling the sheet off the second item, a side table. One by one, Meg exposed the long-forgotten furniture, her smile growing by the minute.

For a brief space of time, she was able to think of Ravensclyde as hers. All the worries, all the heartache of the past year could be pushed away – and hopefully forgotten. Even if it wasn't, Ravensclyde was giving Meg the time she needed to right her crumbling world.

She took the noon meal in the tower room so she could continue looking over her findings. Some were crumbling into dust, and others were too chipped or faded to put out. Already Meg knew where she would put the wardrobe, three side tables, a landscape painting, two tapestries, and a bench.

There was a settee with three matching chairs she was considering having recovered to put in the parlor to brighten up the room.

With the last bite in her mouth, Meg dusted off her hands and stood to wander around the pieces. She had hoped to find more – and Aunt Tilly had led her to believe there was much more – but she would make do with the few items she had found.

She would have repairs started on the others immediately. There was history in all of the pieces, and she wanted to see all of it every day.

Meg walked around a buffet table that needed to be sanded down and repainted. She took a step back to get a better view of the side, and ran into the wall.

And heard the click of a door latch.

She immediately turned to see that a door had come open. A door she had been too busy looking at furniture to notice.

Meg pushed open the door and leaned her head inside. A slow smile spread over her face when she saw another room, twice the size of the one she was just in, and filled with more covered furniture.

Immediately she began to move from piece to piece uncovering them. It wasn't until she neared the far left corner that she spotted a tall covered piece set aside, as if separated from the rest.

Curious, Meg walked toward it. With each step, a prickling stole over her skin that was a peculiar and exciting mixture of foreboding and anticipation.

When she lifted her hand to grasp the sheet, she found it shaking.

Suddenly, the tower was too quiet, the room too still. She forced a laugh, hoping the sound of her own voice would help calm her.

It didn't.

"How silly I'm being," she said aloud and swallowed. "I wanted to be here by myself."

Meg took a deep breath once she realized how foolish she was being. And with a yank, pulled down the sheet.

To find a huge mirror.

It might look like a mirror, but it couldn't be because it didn't reflect her or her surroundings. There was nothing but darkness in the glass. It gaped around her, seeming to suck all the light from the room.

Meg shivered and hastily threw the sheet back over the mirror before she ran out of the tower as if flames were licking at her heels.

~ ~ ~

Ronan opened his eyes. For just a moment he could have sworn he saw light. When only the blackness met his gaze, he realized he must have been dreaming of sunshine.

Again.

How much time had passed? There was no way to tell, and he probably didn't want to know. It seemed lifetimes ago that he had stood with his friends in a gypsy camp eager to ease the ache of his cock between Ana's beautiful thighs.

Twice before he had been let out of the mirror. The first time he had been so shocked he hadn't realized what was going on. The woman had been startled by his sudden appearance and ran screaming from the room.

Ronan had taken his chance and climbed out the window, scaled the wall of the castle, and started running across the countryside.

He got away. Or so he thought. Two days later, he woke up back in that room with the female staring down at him angrily. Next to her was an old woman who had the dark eyes of a gypsy.

Ronan had reached out his hand, in the middle of begging them to let him stay, when the mirror sucked him back in.

The second time, he was more prepared. As soon as he was thrown out of the mirror, he gave the young lass a charming smile.

She was a rather plain female, but the seduction that had always come easy to him failed, as she hastily sent him back. That's how he discovered it was a mirror he was in. And that the mirror belonged to the Alpin family.

Both times he had been in Scotland, but a quick glance at the women's clothes told him that a considerable space of time had passed in both incidences.

Ronan let out a loud sigh and closed his eyes again. He wondered where his friends were, what they were doing, and how they had lived their lives.

Were they dead? Had they found wives? Did they have children?

Had they tried to find him?

He knew the answer to his last question. Of course they had. Morcant, Daman, and Stefan were his brothers. Not once had any of them not been there for the others.

Ronan wished he could let them know he was all right. Maybe they could figure out how to free him. Magic might have put him here, but the old gypsy had told him there was a way to earn his freedom.

He didn't realize until it was too late how he had taken everything for granted. The sunlight, the taste of food, staring at the moon, swimming the cold waters of the loch, making love to a pretty lass, the excitement of battle, or just sharing a dram of whisky with his friends.

The darkness he was bound to had brought to light one thing – he should have handled Ana better.

So many times he had gone over that night in his head and said something different, done something different. His abhorrence to wanting a wife was not Ana's fault. She might have blindsided him with her question of marriage, but he shouldn't have been so callous.

It never entered his mind that she would kill herself. She was young and beautiful, holding an allure only a gypsy could.

She claimed to love him, and once he had said

no to marriage, she took her life. All his dealings with love had proven it wasn't worth pursuing.

Another lesson learned, and one he'd known before Ana. His mother and sister had taught him all too well.

Ronan rubbed a hand down his face. At least in the cursed mirror he didn't have to worry about shaving, eating, or growing old. It was like all of that had been muted.

The one thing that wasn't muted? His need.

It was agonizing, excruciating to be in such a constant state of arousal with nothing to relieve him. He had tried many times, unsuccessfully, to ease himself. Always he was left wanting, needy.

He didn't know what was worse – the loneliness, or the ever-present craving to ease his heated flesh.

If he ever got the chance to get outside the mirror again, he would do everything in his power to remain and get free of the damn mirror once and for all.

Ronan stilled. Was that...could it be...

He opened his eyes and gasped when he saw the light shining through the mirror. He sat up and stood, the light beckoning him. Ronan was powerless to ignore it, not that he would.

His one thought, one goal was to get out of the mirror once and for all. The old gypsy had gotten her wish. He had atoned for what happened to Ana. Now it was time to live his life.

When Ronan reached the light, he tried to step through the mirror, but he couldn't. He didn't know what had to happen to pull him out. All he knew was that it wasn't happening now.

He was getting a peek at the light and a room he didn't recognize. There was no one in sight, no Alpin woman who had summoned him.

At least that's what he assumed took place. Then again, he knew next to nothing about what was going on with the mirror or how it was connected to him.

Ronan put his hand against the invisible barrier that kept him in his dark prison. The light touched his skin, the heat of it sinking into his pores and racing along his hand to his arm and then over his body.

How he longed to bask in the sun, to stand beneath the moon, to feel the rain upon his skin.

A soft, very feminine sigh broke him from his thoughts. Ronan's breath caught in his lungs. He silently prayed and begged to any deity who would listen to let him out of the mirror.

He searched for the woman to no avail. He couldn't see her, but she was near. Whatever was covering the mirror had slid part-ways off.

"I can't," said a female voice laced with a Scottish brogue. "I can't look in that mirror again."

The barrier holding Ronan evaporated, sending him face-first against the wooden boards of a floor. His arms caught himself before his face could hit. He stood, scrambling away from the mirror and looking around.

He immediately went to the window. Ronan took in a deep breath and closed his eyes as the sunlight hit his face.

Free at last.

And he was going to make damn sure he stayed that way.

CHAPTER TWO

Meg stared in silent wonder at the man standing before the window, soaking in the sun as if he had never felt its heat before.

His hair was long, falling just past his shoulders, and the color was a deep brown bordering on black. Even from his profile she could see the hard line of his jaw. Her eyes drifted lower and her heart slammed into her ribcage. The man wore no shirt with his kilt, displaying an abundance of thick, corded muscles.

Meg pulled her eyes away, but in an instant she was back to staring. His arms hung casually at his sides, but there was nothing cavalier about the man. He was a warrior, a man who went after whatever he wanted – and got it.

She saw the scars covering his torso, proving he

had seen his share of battles. Yet they did nothing to detract from his allure. In fact, his prowess inflamed her blood.

Meg didn't recognize the woman responding so...flagrantly to the stranger. No man had ever made her stomach flutter or her skin dew just thinking about him. Her blood was pounding in her ears, her heart beating fast and furious as her hands itched to run over his body and learn every contour.

Suddenly the man's eyes opened. For several heartbeats he stared out the window. Then, slowly, he turned his head to her.

Meg's breath locked in her lungs and her knees threatened to buckle. If she thought the stranger was appealing before, she was wholly unprepared for when he faced her.

He was Adonis, so blindingly handsome that she couldn't fathom what he was doing in her tower. He was the kind of man women fought over – and killed over. He was the kind of man who looked at anyone but Meg.

And yet, his beautiful pale green eyes were focused directly on her. The dark brown eyebrows slashed fiercely over his eyes, and his nose was slightly crooked from having been broken a time or two. His square jaw and chin only heightened his sexiness. However, it was his wide lips - with the bottom fuller than the top - that made her blood race in her veins.

He embodied virility and masculinity, almost as if he had created the two simply by being born.

"Hello, lass."

The sound of such a smooth, deep voice did something strange and glorious to Meg. Was there nothing about the man she didn't like?

"Who are you?" she managed to ask around her thumping heart.

The stranger gave a slight bow of his head, his gaze never leaving hers. "Ronan Galt, at your service. And you are?"

And she was what? It took a moment for Meg to realize he was asking her name. Could she make a bigger fool of herself? "I'm Meg. Meg Alpin."

"Meg." He said her name slowly, letting it fall from his lips as if a prayer.

At this rate, she would be a puddle of nothing. God help her if he came toward her.

Ronan couldn't take his eyes off the fetching Meg. It could have been because he spent so much time alone in his dark prison, but he found her...refreshing. Her auburn hair, having come loose of its pins, was falling about her face in tempting waves.

He wanted to know how long her hair was. And he wanted to feel it slide through his fingers. As much as her hair tempted him, the woman was simply luscious. She had curves to make a saint's mouth water with desire.

Full breasts, a small waist, and flared hips begged for his touch. Her large, expressive gray eyes watched him like an eagle. With her pert nose, wide forehead, and gently arching auburn brows, she would be an invitation for any man.

But it was her high cheekbones and plump, kissable lips that truly made her a temptation no man could pass up.

Meg. The name suited her. Part imp, part seductress. She could have a man on his knees in a matter of moments if she so wanted. But did she know her power?

By the wariness that stole over her gaze, Ronan realized she didn't. That was fortunate for him.

"How did you get in here?" she asked nervously.

He could listen her to her soft lilt all day. She was temptation in the most beautiful package, and the constant, aching need he'd had for so long was difficult to control.

All Ronan wanted to do was push her against the wall and kiss her inviting lips while removing her gown so he could look his fill at her womanly curves.

"I'm no' sure you'd believe me if I told you."

She raised an auburn brow, anxiety replaced with strength. "Try me."

Ronan glanced at the hated mirror. Everything hinged on getting this beguiling, beautiful woman to believe him and let him remain in her world. If he couldn't, he would be forced back into the hated mirror once more. He had to gain his freedom.

He slowly released a deep breath and motioned to the mirror with his hand. "From there."

The disbelief on Meg's face was just what he expected. "From the mirror?"

"Did you no' pull the sheet down, lass? There

was naught to see, was there? Just blackness, a void that stretched endlessly."

She took a step back, fear and confusion mixing on her lovely face. "I don't understand."

"I didna either for a long time." He'd never had a chance to explain himself before, and he worried he would say the wrong thing. So much had never ridden on so little. "The first Alpin woman who released me sent me back into my prison before I could tell her anything. The second gave me a little more time, but no' much. This is just my third time."

"Alpin?" she asked with a small frown marring her forehead as she looked from him to the mirror and back to him. "My ancestors? That's not possible."

"There is much that is possible with magic."

"Magic?" she repeated, as if testing the word on her lips. For long moments she stared at him as if trying to decide if he was daft or not.

Ronan bit back the words that wanted to tumble from his mouth. He was prepared to fall upon his knees and beg her for at least a full day so he could see the sun and the moon, taste food and ale, and perhaps ease the ache of his cock. Instead, he stood staring at her, silently willing her to give him a chance.

Relief poured through him as she said, "I'm not saying I believe you, but how long have you been in the mirror?"

"What year is it?" he asked, almost afraid to hear the answer.

"1609."

Disappointment speared Ronan. It was as he feared. He hadn't just spent decades in that awful mirror. He had spent centuries.

"Ronan?"

He met her gaze, surprised to find pity in her stormy depths. "Nearly two hundred years it seems."

Silence filled the room as their gazes locked – hers unsure, his accepting. Ronan didn't know if she was attempting to believe him, but it didn't matter. He was taken aback at the fact that his friends, the men he considered brothers, were long dead. He would never see them again, never share a keg of whisky, never ride into battle together.

The sadness that fell over him was debilitating, devastating. Unbearable.

What was he going to do now?

Meg bit her lip as she studied Ronan's face. He was visibly shaken by the realization that two centuries had passed. She wanted to toss him out on his arse for the liar that he was, but the more she watched him, the more she began to believe him.

No one could fake such alarm. As difficult as that was to watch, it was the sorrow, the grief that filled his light green eyes that broke her heart.

"Did you leave a wife behind?" she asked hesitantly.

Ronan shook his head as he turned to stare out the window once more. "Nay. It's my friends I mourn. We were brothers in every sense of the word."

The desolation in his voice made her throat close up with emotion. What did one say in response? She couldn't think of anything that would help.

Meg looked around, her gaze going to the mirror. It had been nothing but blackness when she looked into it before. If...magic...had been used, and he had been stuck in that awful thing for two centuries, she couldn't imagine how he was feeling.

She bit back a snort. Nor could she comprehend that she was even considering his words as truth. He might very well be jesting with her, but the simple fact was that one moment he hadn't been there, and then the next he had.

Magic or not, trickery or not, he was a man who was deep in torment. "Are you hungry?"

A small grin flitted over his lips. "I've no' eaten in so long I no longer remember the taste of food."

"That I can remedy," Meg said with a nod. She had a purpose now. To feed Ronan. That she could do easily enough.

She turned and hurried out of the rooms to the stairway. Halfway down she realized she hadn't asked him to stay put. But then again, where would he go? Back into the mirror?

Meg ordered a tray of food to be brought up to the tower and dashed back up as quickly as she could. She was out of breath by the time she walked into the room.

Her gaze immediately went to the window, but Ronan was nowhere to be found. A quick scan showed nothing. Had he really gone back in the mirror?

Just as she was walking to the object in question, Ronan came out from behind the mirror, his attention focused entirely on the large piece.

"How long has this been in your family?"

Meg shrugged and came to a stop when she realized how close to him she had gotten. Seeing him from a distance was difficult enough, but up close he robbed her of her will. "This isn't my home. It's my great-aunt's. I'm staying for a bit."

At her words, Ronan's green gaze shifted to her. "Why are you no' married? I'd have expected some man to have stolen your heart already."

Meg swallowed and turned to the doorway as memories threatened. "The food will be up soon. As a matter of fact, I think I hear Mary on the stairs."

She fled, like the coward she was, from Ronan and his questions. For a little while, she had forgotten what had sent her to Ravensclyde. Those precious few moments had been amazing.

"Put it here, Mary," Meg directed the maid to a small table more suited for teacups than a large tray filled to the brim with food.

"You barely ate your luncheon, milady," Mary said eyeing the tray.

Meg smiled. "Exactly. I've found my appetite."

"That's good to hear," Mary said with a sigh. "We were most worried about you. You need more meat on that thin frame of yours, milady."

With those words, Mary was gone, leaving Meg

alone with Ronan. Meg wasn't sure why she didn't want anyone else to know about Ronan. Maybe because he could just be a figment of her imagination.

Or it could be that she didn't want to explain how he arrived.

Mostly, she realized it was because she didn't want to share him yet.

"Why are they worried over you, sweet Meg?"

His words, spoken so near her, made her stomach flutter. Meg shifted to the side a couple of steps so she could see him. "I was ill."

"Ill? And they let you up here to sort through these rooms alone?" he asked suspiciously, almost angrily.

Meg pulled up a stool that looked capable of holding Ronan and pointed to the tray. "Please. Eat."

Thankfully his attention was diverted to the food. He inhaled deeply, a smile on his face as he sat. He looked at each item in turn before he reached for the mug of ale. In short order he polished off the entire tray. Meg sat and watched him savor each bite as if he would never eat again.

Once he had finished the last chicken leg, she asked, "How did you get in the mirror?"

There was the slightest pause in his movements as he wiped his hands and mouth. "I'm no' sure it's a story you want to know."

"I assure you it is. The more I know, the better I can make my decision."

"And what will you do with me if you doona

believe me, sweet Meg?" he asked softly, those stunning eyes of his pinning her to the chair. "Will you send me back just to see if you can?"

"I'm not that cruel."

He looked her over and shook his head. "Nay, I doona believe you are."

"It's all just so hard to believe."

At this he snorted. "Hard to believe there's magic? In Scotland? Lass, you should know the mountains are full of it."

"I've never seen magic," she admitted, hating the tremor in her voice.

His head cocked to the side. "Did you look in my mirror today?"

"Aye."

"Did you see your reflection?"

"I did not."

"That is because magic was used to give you a glimpse into my prison."

"That place scares me."

He sighed and reached for the ale. Just before he brought the mug to his lips he said, "It's good at doing that."

CHAPTER THREE

Ronan no more wanted to talk about what had happened that fateful night – two hundred years ago – than he wanted to think about it. But if he was going to be free from the damned mirror, he had to convince Meg never to send him back.

He could try to lie to her, but he had a feeling the woman would know immediately. That only left the truth – as hard as it was to acknowledge.

"I was with my friends, Daman, Morcant, and Stefan," he said. "Though we were all from different clans, we were together more than we were apart. If one of us needed something, the other three would be there."

Meg's lips turned up in a small smile. "That sounds nice. I've never had anything like that."

"I took it for granted, just as I did everything

else." Damn. Those words were more truth than he had ever acknowledged, even to himself. "I loved to have fun, and took advantage of every opportunity that presented itself. When a band of gypsies came to the land of Daman's clan, I was the first to visit."

"Why?" Meg asked, her brow knitted in confusion. "Did you want your fortune told?"

Ronan drained the last of the ale from the goblet and gently set it down. "A woman caught my eye. With her black hair and eyes, her dark skin, and the vibrant colors she wore, she was stunning."

"Ah. I see."

"I wasna a man to take a woman's innocence," Ronan stated when he saw the condemnation on Meg's face. "Ana wasna an innocent. I didna force her either."

"Nay, I don't imagine you had to. I'm sure she was as enamored with your good looks as you were with her."

Ronan shrugged. "Regardless, we found pleasure in each other's arms. I would come to her at night, and leave before the dawn. I assumed our relationship was one of mutual pleasure and nothing more."

"But she wanted more," Meg guessed.

"That she did." Ronan set his hands on his legs and sighed. "On that last night, I brought my friends with me to partake in what the gypsies freely offered. It had never entered my mind that Ana would assume I wanted her as my wife."

Meg's face scrunched up, something haunted

and broken flashing in her gray eyes. "You broke her heart."

Ronan stood and walked around the room amidst the furniture. "I told her there would be no marriage between us. When that didna stop her words, I thought a small lie would. I told her I was already promised to another. She ran crying from the wagon."

"I take it the gypsies weren't happy?"

"I doona think I'll ever know. I was getting ready to leave the camp when I heard a scream. I jumped out of the wagon ready to defend the gypsies when I saw Ana. She had taken her own life. Because I wouldna marry her."

Meg wiped at a strand of hair tickling her cheek. "The gypsies cursed you, didn't they?"

"The old woman did. I think she might have been Ana's grandmother. She sent me into the black void. I didna realize it was a mirror until the second time I was released."

"Are you cursed to remain in the mirror forever?"

Ronan turned and faced her. "The old woman said I would be in there until I earned my freedom."

"What does that mean?" Meg asked as she leaned forward.

"It means, sweet Meg, that if you doona send me back, I'll be free."

Her back straightened. "Oh. Is that all? Fine. I won't send you back."

Ronan nearly shouted with joy. It hadn't taken

nearly as much effort on his part to convince Meg as he thought it might. He'd felt the sun, had a delicious meal, and no longer had the mirror to worry about.

Best of all, he had engaged in conversation with a most enticingly beautiful woman. And he found himself hungry for something else.

"Why are you here, Meg?"

Suddenly twitchy, she rose to her feet and shrugged. "I needed a place to think. Aunt Tilly offered Ravensclyde, and I accepted the invitation. Now, back to you. What are you going to do?"

"Do?" Ronan hadn't thought about that. His attention had been focused on getting free, not what would happen once he did. He expected it to take days - weeks even - to convince Meg to release him.

It had gone frighteningly easy. That sent a niggle of worry down his spine. Nothing that came easy was good.

Ronan pushed that concern to the side for a moment. With Stefan, Daman, and Morcant dead, there was no one for him to find. And nowhere for him to go.

He was homeless, penniless, and friendless. A hell of a problem to find himself in. Then he looked at Meg again, an idea taking root. "Do you need help around the castle?"

Her mouth twisted as she shook her head. "Not really." She paused as if considering his words. "Then again, you don't know anyone or the times. I'm not sure I should just let you go out on your own."

"I'll be fine, I assure you."

"Things are different than when you knew them."

Ronan smiled. "So you believe my tale, sweet Meg."

"I'm not saying that," she replied saucily. "But I'm leaning in that direction. Too much doesn't add up. Your tartan is an old weave for one."

He closed the distance between them and smiled when he realized he had her backed against the chair with nowhere to run. "Where is your man, sweet Meg?"

Her gaze darted away before coming back to his. He made her nervous, and by the rapid pulse beat at the base of her neck and the way her eyes darkened when she looked at him, her body had a reaction to him.

"I don't have a man," she said in a husky whisper.

Ronan's gaze dropped to her lips. They would taste as sweet as wine. "Their loss."

Meg slipped to the side and backed away from Ronan. He was more than temptation. He was sin, begging her to sample what he offered.

And did she ever want a taste of it.

"If you're in need of a woman, I'm sure you'll find plenty willing to accommodate you throughout the castle."

Ronan's smile was predatory, as if he knew she wanted to give in to the desires heating her body. If he only knew just how much she yearned to do just that.

"How will you explain my appearance?" he asked.

Meg grimaced. "I don't know yet. You can't just come down with me."

"Why no'?"

Why not, indeed? She was in charge of the castle for the moment. Already a story was forming about Ronan, clarifying his position as someone who just arrived seeking work. It wasn't a lie. She just wouldn't tell anyone he came from a mirror.

"You can remain for as long as you need. During that time, you may help around the castle. Follow me, and I'll introduce you to everyone."

She turned on her heel and walked out of the room to the stairs. Ronan was one step behind her. His presence was comforting, even as he put her on edge.

~ ~ ~

Days turned into weeks, and during that time Ronan thought of Meg, of leaning over her, her soft curves cushioning him before he thrust inside her. There was something very compelling about her. Ronan couldn't pinpoint exactly what it was, but he knew it was more about the woman herself than the fact he had been alone for so long.

He hungered for food and the pleasures of the flesh.

He craved the feel of the rain upon his skin.

He yearned for the sun and the wind.

But Meg's presence dimmed everything else.

There was pain in her gray eyes, but the light within her brightened all. She was tempting, arousing, and fierce without even knowing it.

Ronan had been given odd jobs throughout the castle. The fact there wasn't much for him to do showed how well run the castle truly was.

He would often find himself near Meg, and he used every opportunity to speak with her in the hopes of learning more about her. Each time he made her laugh was a small triumph.

As the days flew by, he found himself searching for her to make sure she was within reach and safe. When he wasn't checking on Meg, he was working outside any chance he got so he could bask in the sun.

It had felt good to use his muscles and his mind. How he used to complain about the menial work his uncle made him perform. Wouldn't his uncle be laughing now if he could see that Ronan was looking for work to occupy him.

A month to the day that he had been freed from his prison, he waited for Meg. Three nights in a row he had woken with a feeling that he needed to go to the mirror, and every night that feeling increased. It unsettled him, because he feared he might not have a choice of remainin and making a life. He could be back in the hated mirror regardless of what Meg said.

He pushed away from the wall and smiled when he spotted her walking from the castle with a basket laden with food. He quickly fell into step beside her. "Need some help?"

He didn't give her time to answer as he took the basket. Her strides were long and purposeful as her gaze darted to the ominous clouds that filled the sky.

"Did you sleep well?" she asked as she nodded in passing to a man tending to the horses.

"I didna sleep." Even in the night he was battered on all sides by the sounds and sights around him. It was so different than the silent blackness he had known for so long. As he soaked it all in, sleep was the farthest thing from his mind.

His chamber – on an opposite side of the castle from Meg's – had a lovely view. Yet, he found himself standing outside her door most nights fighting his desire to taste her lips and skin. He wouldn't go uninvited into her room when she was offering him a roof over his head, food in his stomach, and most especially, freedom from the mirror.

But how he hungered for her.

So much so, that when he had found a willing woman, he had walked away. Him. Walked away! It unheard of. Particularly when his cock ached for relief.

The maid's kisses had been experienced, her body soft, but she hadn't been Meg. Even now he couldn't believe he had left a willing female to instead stand guard outside Meg's door with desire burning through him.

She frowned as she cut her eyes to him. "Aren't you tired?"

"When there is only darkness around you, there's no need to open your eyes. I feel as if I've slept away years. I want to take it all in while I have the chance."

"You still think I'm going to send you back," she said, appalled. "I said I wouldn't."

He shrugged. It wasn't like Ronan could tell her he didn't trust women. He knew them to be manipulative, devious creatures who wanted nothing more than their own pleasures.

Meg came to a halt. It took a moment for Ronan to realize that she had stopped, so he was a couple of paces ahead before he paused and turned to look at her.

Her gray eyes blazed with fury as the wind whipped at the strands of her auburn hair that had come loose of the simple braid. "You think I'm lying. Me!"

Ronan shifted the basket to his other hand and braced himself. First there was anger, and then women cried. He hoped Meg wouldn't shed any tears. It would ruin everything. "Two other women have sent me back."

"I don't know how I called you out of the mirror, so it just goes to show that I don't know how to send you back. Plus I told you I wouldn't. Obviously, you take a woman's word as nothing."

"It was a woman who put me in the mirror."

Meg's eyes widened in annoyance. "Oh, well then never mind that you refused to wed her granddaughter after bedding her."

"I didna kill Ana," Ronan said in a low voice.

He was surprised at the anger that rose up so quickly. He was many things, but he wasn't a murderer.

The ire evaporated from Meg's face instantly. "You're right. You didn't. Ana was weak. Men regularly go back on vows and seduce women with false promises, and we survive. Ana should have as well. Men aren't worth the time, and they certainly aren't worth our souls."

Ronan could only stare after Meg as she walked past him onto the worn road from the castle. There had been something in her voice, a note of regret and desolation that was like a sword through his gut.

He wanted to know what had happened to her, but more than that, he wanted to know who had hurt her. She was a gentle spirit, but he had glimpsed the fire and passion in her gaze. She was a beauty waiting to break through the chains holding her back.

With little effort, Ronan caught up with Meg. They walked in silence for a while. He kept going over what she had said in his mind. There was no doubt some man had forsaken her. Had he stolen her innocence and refused to marry her?

The idea made Ronan grip the handle of the basket so hard that it creaked in protest. Gradually, he loosened his hand until he had his rage under control.

"You doona trust men," he said into the silence. "Why are you trusting me, lass?"

She looked at him with wide gray eyes and

smiled tightly. "Oh, I don't."

"I doona understand. Why let me have my freedom then? Why allow me to sleep in the castle, to work and eat there?"

They came to a small rundown cottage, and Meg stopped and reached into the basket. "You didn't hurt me, Ronan, and everyone needs a second chance to build their lives."

"Is that what you're doing? Building your life?"

She laughed, but the sound was forced. "Nay. Mine was over before it ever began."

He could only watch as she knocked on the cottage door and handed cheese and a loaf of bread to a woman so bent with age she couldn't stand straight.

There were no more words as he walked beside her to the next cottage where five small children gathered around her before she could even get to the door.

The pleasure on her face as she interacted with them was evident. Meg was a woman made to be a mother. She nourished and encouraged as if it were second nature. And the children responded to her.

For once, he was looking at a woman as something more than a source of pleasure. He was seeing Meg, really seeing her. It was something new, and it felt as if the earth had been yanked out from beneath him.

Women were all the same. Weren't they?

Weeks ago he would have said yes, but after meeting Meg and coming to know her, he was reevaluating his ideas. She hadn't manipulated him into giving her anything. She hadn't cried or used her body.

She had, however, given him the one thing he wanted above all – freedom. While asking for nothing in return.

Was that why he felt compelled to remain near her? Was that why he desired her as deeply as he did?

She may have acted differently than any other woman he knew, but he wasn't yet convinced that she wouldn't become what he had learned women truly were.

Still...he couldn't stop thinking about Meg.

Ronan propped a hip against the stone wall surrounding the cottage. The roof was in desperate need of repair, and the stack of wood for the fire only had a few logs left. As he catalogued what needed to be done, he took note of how Meg gave a treat to each child that sent them running around the yard with bright smiles and laughter.

By the time Meg rejoined him, a serene smile was in place.

"What?" she asked when she saw him staring.

"You should have children of your own."

She licked her lips and brushed past him to continue on the road without responding.

"Do you deny you want children?" he asked, unsure why it seemed so important to him.

"Nay."

That one word held a wealth of meaning – fear, pain. But more than that, there was resignation.

CHAPTER FOUR

Meg was surprised Ronan joined her as she visited the sick tenants. She hated the way her body responded to him, loathed how she tried to brush against him in any effort to feel him. She was pathetic in her need to be near him, and yet she refused to send him away.

As if he would do what she wanted. Ronan was stubborn and thick headed. He would do whatever it was he wished. She was thrilled that for the moment she was some kind of fascination for him. It wouldn't last, which was why she would soak it up now.

Her arm heated where she knew his gaze landed. The heat traveled to her neck, and then to her chest. Her breasts swelled and her nipples tightened. Just knowing he was watching her made her heartbeat accelerate.

"Where are the parents from the last cottage we visited?" he asked.

Meg swallowed twice, trying to get moisture back to her mouth. She was grateful for the change of subject. She didn't want to think about her life without a husband or children. All she had ever wanted was a family of her own to cherish.

"Their mother died last winter trying to bring another babe into the world. The babe didn't make it either. The father was desolate after his wife died, which is understandable. He spent his nights drinking away his pain. It caused him to fall and break his ankle when he was trying to bring in some sheep."

"How long until he gets back on his feet?"

Meg gave a little shrug. "A few more weeks. I know there is a young girl from a neighboring cottage that comes over when she can to cook and look after the young ones."

Ronan nodded as he listened, his gaze intent upon the road before them.

She darted her gaze to him. He might be willing to do common work, but there was nothing common about Ronan. He stood straight and powerful, commanding and forceful. It was obvious that he was used to being in control.

"Who were you?" Meg asked. "Before the curse. What did you do?"

He laughed and glanced at her. "I did what any good Highlander does, lass. I fought my enemies and protected my clan."

"But who were you? You walk like a man used to being in charge, a man who made his own rules."

"That's because I did." He gave her a crooked smile to ease the harshness of his words.

Meg was more curious than ever. She didn't recognize the tartan he wore, but clans would subtly change their plaids for reasons like banishments, marriages, and such.

She watched Ronan out of the corner of her eye. There was no denying his confidence, his air of authority. No man, not even a Highlander, got that without being born into it.

"You were no crofter's son," Meg said. "You were son to the laird."

If she hadn't been looking for any reaction, Meg would have missed the slight tightening of his muscles.

"A good guess, but no' quite true."

"It makes sense," she stated.

Ronan pierced her with his pale green eyes. "So it would seem."

"Why do you want to hide that fact?"

"I wasna the laird's son. I was his nephew. And it's a good thing my father wasna laird. My mother had him twisted around her finger so tightly all he could see was her."

Meg swallowed at the hatred she heard in Ronan's voice, though she wasn't sure if it was toward his mother or father. She guessed it was because of his mother. "Is that why you disdain women so much?"

Her question caused him to throw back his head and laugh. "Disdain? Lass, I love women. Why do you think I was cursed?"

Meg took the trail branching off from the road, undeterred by his words. His laugh was too loud, too long. "You despise women. You regard us as a means to ease your body, but you find no other need for us."

She stopped him with a hand on his arm before he could respond. After taking a loaf of bread and meat wrapped in a towel, Meg made her way to the door of the cottage.

This was the only place Aunt Tilly had begged her to visit daily. Not that the old woman who lived there ever said much to Meg, but it was such a small request.

Meg gave a sharp knock, only to have the door open immediately. She smiled, noting how the black eyes of the woman stared at her for long moments before looking over her shoulder to Ronan.

"This will get you through tomorrow, Ina," Meg said as she handed over the items. "Cook is making soup, and I'll be sure to have some brought over for you."

Ina's gaze came back to her before she promptly closed the door in Meg's face. With a shrug, Meg turned and walked back to Ronan.

"Who is that woman?" he asked.

Meg glanced over her shoulder to the cottage to find Ina peering at them from her window. "I don't really know. She's important to Aunt Tilly. Why?"

"She has the look of a gypsy about her."

They spent the rest of the morning in companionable silence visiting the remaining cottages. By the time the basket was empty, thunder was rumbling at a steady rate.

"I doona think we'll make it back to the castle before it rains."

Meg sighed loudly. "I was hoping we would, but we have at least three miles to walk before we get to the castle."

"Why no' take a horse. It would be quicker."

"It would, but I like to walk."

There was another rumble of thunder before a crack of lightning made Meg jump. Not a heartbeat later it began to rain.

"Is there shelter nearby?" Ronan asked.

Meg knew of only one. The abandoned cottage deep in the woods. "Aye. I'll show you."

She took off at a run. To her surprise, Ronan grabbed her hand as she lifted her sodden skirts and dashed into the forest. She slipped on damp leaves and earth, but Ronan easily kept her on her feet.

A laugh escaped her. For the first time in...years...she felt lighthearted and...free. It was a glorious feeling.

Meg looked up through the trees at the rain falling and never saw the rock. Both legs came out from beneath her. A cry welled up in her throat, and just as suddenly, she was hauled against a rock-hard chest.

She didn't know how much time passed as she

stared at Ronan's bare chest. When she did look up into his eyes, there was a fire burning there.

It caused her heart to skip a beat and something seductive and erotic unfurl low in her belly.

But it frightened her too.

The stark desire was there for her to see. Ronan held nothing back. There were no false words, no lies, no empty promises.

There was just him.

His hand settled on her chest above her breasts, and then he slowly caressed up her neck to cup her cheek. All the while his head lowered to hers.

Meg should turn away. She knew it, but her body wouldn't listen. Ronan only wanted to ease his own desires. He cared nothing for her.

What does it matter? Why can't I have such pleasure in my miserable life?

As soon as the thought flitted through her mind, the last vestiges of her restraint vanished. Meg watched the water run down the hard planes of Ronan's face. She parted her lips and let her eyes drift shut. The first brush of his mouth against hers was but a touch. The second was more purposeful, as he pressed his lips to hers.

Meg could feel herself melting against him. Then his tongue slid along the seam of her lips. She gasped, her fingers digging into his shoulders.

It was the moan, the hard, needy moan pulled from deep within him that left her trembling for more. When he turned her slightly in his arms and opened his lips wider, Meg followed suit.

She sighed as their tongues met, tangled. The

attraction between them exploded into hot flames of desire. He deepened the kiss, pulling her against him until she could feel his arousal.

The kiss was searing, scorching. It burned her from the inside out.

And she couldn't get enough.

It was hard for her to hide the disappointment when Ronan ended the kiss and stared down at her. Without a word, he took her hand and walked her to the abandoned cottage.

As soon as he stepped into the structure, he pulled her inside and shut the door. In the next instant, he had her pressed against the door, his mouth on hers again, more ravenous than before.

Meg slid her arms around his neck and sank her fingers into the thick strands of his wet hair. The kiss stirred her already heated blood. She gasped when he rocked against her, his thick rod pressing against her sex.

"Aye," he murmured as he kissed down her neck. "Feel me, sweet Meg."

She felt the cool air on her skin, and realized he was undressing her, but she no longer cared. All she wanted was more of the pleasure Ronan was giving her. She would think about her actions and the consequences later.

Now was all about what she wanted.

It was a new sensation for her. Never had she thought of herself before anyone else, and she found she quite liked it.

Her gown fell around her feet in a flurry of material. Ronan never stopped kissing her the entire time he was getting her naked. When Meg was completely nude, Ronan pulled her against him and looked into her eyes for long moments. She wished she knew what he was thinking, that she had some hint of what went on in his mind.

"I didna lie, sweet Meg. I've never taken an innocent before."

She might have blushed before, but not now. Not when her body ached for him. His large hands were roaming over her, gripping her bottom and teasing the undersides of her breasts.

"You don't bed virgins, remember. What makes you think I'm an innocent?" she asked, her voice shaking when he drew close to her already hard nipple.

"A man like me always knows."

Her lids drifted shut when she ground against him. "I don't need to be seduced. I'm more than willing."

"I should walk away from you, from this."

Meg's eyes flew open to see him staring down at her breasts. He had bent her backward, exposing her breasts. She couldn't imagine him leaving her in such a state of need. Besides, she knew he needed release as well.

"Don't." Meg didn't care that he heard the pleading in her voice. "Please."

He drew his gaze up to hers. "You doona know what you're asking."

But she did. To prove it, she reached between them and wrapped her hand around his cock. "I know."

With her words, Ronan unfastened his kilt and let it drop to the ground. He knelt in front of Meg and cupped her breasts in his hands before he closed his mouth over one turgid peak.

Ronan had never wanted a woman like he wanted Meg. He teased her nipples mercilessly until her hips were rocking against him. Only then did he take the precious few moments to spread his kilt over the dirt floor and lay her down.

That's when he finally got to feast his eyes on Meg in all her glorious splendor. Her nipples were a pale pink, her breasts large and full. She had a narrow waist and full hips. He glanced at her lithe legs, but it was the triangle of auburn curls between them that held him transfixed.

"You are a beauty, sweet Meg."

Her smile was soft, seductive, and it caused a bolt of need to rush through Ronan. She had no idea of her appeal. He knelt between her legs and leaned over her to kiss her again.

Their limbs tangled as they rolled about touching and learning each other while soft sighs and moans filled the cottage.

Ronan couldn't get enough of her. He fondled her breasts before caressing one hand down her stomach to her sex. He groaned when he found her already wet and ready. Sliding one finger inside her, he was rewarded when she moaned and arched against him.

While he continued to thrust his finger in and out of her tight sheath, he rubbed his thumb around her swollen clit. Her moans turned into cries of pleasure. Every time lightning lit up the sky he was shown a vision of pure eroticism.

Ronan felt her body stiffen, and knew she was close to peaking. He continued his assault, adding a second finger to the first. Then, he leaned down and gently bit a nipple before flicking his tongue over it.

She came apart with a scream, the walls of her sex clenching his finger. And it was the most beautiful thing Ronan had ever seen.

CHAPTER FIVE

Meg didn't know her body could feel so good or be taken so high. She opened her eyes as Ronan pulled his fingers from her body. He was leaning over her, the head of his cock at the entrance to her sex.

She knew why he hesitated, and it made her smile. Meg rested her hands on his sides and urged him to her. His pale green eyes widened in surprise.

And then he was pushing inside her, stretching her, filling her. Meg lifted her legs and was amazed when he slid deeper. He paused, and withdrew until just the tip of him was inside her.

With one thrust, he pushed through her maidenhead, burying himself fully.

Meg stiffened at the pain, but it wasn't long until it diminished. Then something primal, something ancient had her moving against him. As soon as she felt him slide in and out of her, the pleasure, when it returned, was amplified.

She gave herself up to the rhythm Ronan set. The tempo increased as he went deeper, thrust harder. And each time the pleasure low in her belly tightened.

Her second climax was as fierce as the first, sweeping her away on a ride of ecstasy. She knew in that instant that her body belonged to Ronan. He had marked her without even meaning to.

He threw back his head and gave a shout just as he pulled out of her. Meg held him when he collapsed on top of her, his body jerking. That's when she realized he had poured his seed on her stomach.

Meg smoothed his hair back from his face and closed her eyes as she enjoyed the feel of his weight atop her. No one had ever touched her as deeply as Ronan had.

She wasn't the naïve girl this time. This time she knew exactly what he offered – nothing.

Ronan rose up on an elbow and placed a gentle kiss on her mouth before he stood. He tore a part of her chemise off before tearing that section in two. When he returned, he knelt and wiped her blood from between her legs and then his seed from her belly.

With the storm still raging outside, Ronan lay down beside her and pulled her into his arms. Meg welcomed the respite and nestled against him with her head upon his chest.

"Will you tell me what happened to send you to Ravensclyde, sweet Meg?"

His voice was a whisper, barely heard above the rain. But heard it she had. Her eyes opened and she stared at the wall of the cottage. "Will you tell me why you hate women?"

"I doona think it a tale worth telling, but if you want to know, I will tell you."

She shifted her head until she was looking at him. "I want to know."

"All right," he said with a shrug of one shoulder. He tucked his free hand behind his head and looked at the ceiling. "My father fell madly in love with my mother the first time he saw her. What he didna know is that she was trying to win my uncle's attention. Uncle had already married and wasna interested. My father worked twice as hard to win her favor."

"I gather he did," Meg said.

"Unfortunately. My mother used him. She told him she loved him, but it was only to get him to marry her. She made his life hell. Nothing he ever did was good enough. She turned a proud man into a shell of what he once was."

Meg swallowed, because it all became clear to her. It wasn't that Ronan hated women. He didn't believe in love. Add that to the cunning way his mother tricked his father and ruined his life, and it was no wonder Ronan had balked at marriage to the gypsy.

"My sister learned from our mother," Ronan continued. "She was just as scheming and unscrupulous when she was trying to get what she wanted. I tried to warn her husband, but he was too enamored with her to listen. He learned soon enough. But by then it was too late. He was in the same trap as my father."

Meg laid her head back on his chest. "I'm sorry, Ronan."

"It's in the past."

"But still ruling your life," she pointed out.

She closed her eyes as silence stretched between them only broken by the rain and thunder. Meg was almost asleep when his fingers brushed across her cheek to move away her hair.

"I've shared my story. Where is yours?" he asked in a low, husky voice that sent chills racing over her skin.

Meg drew in a deep breath and slowly released it. "There's nothing really to tell. I was given a promise. The promise was broken, leaving me betrayed and alone."

Ronan knew there was much more to the story. He might not know Meg's past, but he knew enough of her to know that she was a good, sweet soul. Whoever had hurt her should be hung up by his balls.

Suddenly, Ronan wanted to look into her gray eyes. He rolled her onto her back so that he leaned on one forearm beside her. Her gaze met his without hesitation.

"Tell me," he urged.

She looked away, all emotion draining from her face. "I met a man I thought cared for me. He told me he wanted me to be his. He even asked me to marry him. I was overjoyed. He was very handsome and charming. My family liked him as well. I thought everything was going along fine."

When she fell silent once more, Ronan ran a finger between her breasts to her navel. "What did he do?"

"He left me. Abandoned me on the day of our wedding to run away with someone else. I've never felt such shame."

"You doona have reason to be ashamed, sweet Meg. He was the fool who let you go. You should be happy no' to be shackled to a man like that."

Her gaze swung back to him. "You're right. Had it not happened, Aunt Tilly wouldn't have offered Ravensclyde to me, and I wouldn't have found you."

"You freed me." The impact of what she had done for him, and given him, slammed into his chest like a battering ram.

"And you awakened my body," she said with a sly smile.

If only she knew how wonderful her body was. It might have been a long time since he'd had a woman, but he knew the pleasure he found with Meg was profound.

Enough to make him think about running as far away as he could.

What stopped him was realizing Meg wasn't like his mother or sister. She had been abandoned by a man. She was wounded, her heart sore. And yet she had given him her most precious gift — her innocence.

No other man had touched her, kissed her, loved her as he had. It was a first for Ronan, and he quite liked how it felt.

"What a pair we are," Meg said with a small laugh.

Ronan rolled to his back. "Aye. A pair for sure."

Meg returned to her spot on his chest. "How long will you stay at Ravensclyde?"

"I've no' thought much about it. Why? Do you wish me to leave now?"

"On the contrary. I want you to stay as long as you want."

Ronan idly played with the drying strands of hair that had come loose from her braid. "I doona understand why you gave yourself to me. That man was an arse to be sure, but you will make a good wife and mother."

"I am the second of four daughters. My father gave my intended the dowry before the wedding."

"And the bastard ran off with it."

"Aye. My sisters need to find husbands as well. There's nothing left for me to find another husband with."

Ronan soaked in that bit of news. "What about your aunt? Can she no' help?"

"She did. She allowed me to come here and make it my home. At least I have somewhere to go that isn't the convent."

"So you've resigned yourself to being alone?"

"I have."

Ronan didn't quite understand why the thought of Meg with another man made him want to hit something, but he also knew Meg shouldn't be alone.

~ ~ ~

Meg wondered if everyone would be able to tell she was no longer a maiden as she and Ronan walked back to the castle once the storm had passed.

When no one looked twice at her, she relaxed. No matter how wrong it was, she couldn't berate herself for what she had done. For those few moments, she had been worshipped, needed, and loved. It went a long way to bolster her failing self-esteem.

Just before they reached the castle, Ronan stopped her with a hand upon her arm. "Is all well?"

"Aye," she said with a smile.

"You're glowing, lass." There was a very male smile pulling at his lips. "I did that to you."

She playfully rolled her eyes. "So you did. I suppose I should thank you."

"Oh, but you did. With a most precious gift," he said in a low whisper.

Meg shivered as she always did when he talked in that husky, seductive voice. "I must go. There are things I need to tend to. Will you be at dinner?"

"Aye."

Ronan watched her walk into the castle before

he strode into the stables and gathered the tools he would need. With his arms full, he was about to head out on foot when the stable master stepped in front of him.

"Where are you headed with those?" the man asked.

Ronan nodded in approval of the man. "I'm off to one of the cottages to make some repairs."

The man eyed him for a few moments before he let out a whistle and a white gelding ran up to the fence. "Take a mount. You'll get there faster."

"Thank you."

"How long will you be staying at Ravensclyde?"

Ronan stopped on his way around the man. "I doona know."

"Where did you come from?"

It wasn't like Ronan could get upset with the man. He was looking out for Meg and the castle. "Somewhere far away. Meg has offered for me to rest at the castle for a while. I want to pay her back by helping out where I can."

The old man's blue gaze went to the castle. "She came here several months ago heart sore. I've no' seen a true smile from her before today."

"I've no intention of hurting Meg if that's what you're asking," Ronan said. "She should be protected. It's good that she has someone like you looking out for her."

The stable master gave a nod of his head and disappeared back into the stables. Ronan quickly grabbed a halter and readied the horse. With his tools in hand, he mounted and rode out of the bailey.

For once, he knew exactly what he needed to do.

CHAPTER SIX

Meg found herself searching for a glimpse of Ronan throughout the rest of the day. Disappointment filled her when she couldn't find him. And a part of her worried that he had left.

"It's not like he promised he would stay," she told herself.

Ronan had given no promises, nor would he ever. After he told her what happened to him, she knew without a doubt that he would remain for only as long as he wished. Afterward, she would never see him again.

Meg's mind was so full of Ronan that she couldn't concentrate on the chores she needed to get done. Her body still hungered for more of him, but there was something else on her mind, something she was afraid to let linger.

Ronan had made sure not to plant his seed within her. She hadn't thought much about it at the time, but now...now she knew he might be the only way she could have the family she wanted.

Meg ran the back of her hand across her forehead as she helped stir the boiling water for the washing. Her time at Ravensclyde was limited to the remainder of Aunt Tilly's life. Once she died, the castle would pass to her eldest son. Even though he had his own castle to manage, Meg was sure he wouldn't be too happy with her remaining forever.

Eventually, Meg was going to have to leave, and even if she could convince Ronan to give her a child, there was nowhere for them to go. Meg was fully dependent on her family, and with no dowry, she could very well end up in a convent.

The thought chilled her.

It always had, but now, more than ever, the reality of her future was weighing heavily upon her shoulders. If only she could decide her own fate.

Meg finished with the laundry and went into the castle. She was in her chamber when she glanced out her window and spotted Ronan talking to the stable master. Her heart immediately began to pound at the sight of such a man, a man she knew to have gentle, loving hands that wrung multitudes of pleasure from her.

The conversation done, Ronan turned to a water barrel and dunked his head. He flipped his head back, water flying everywhere, as a huge smile graced his handsome face.

Meg glanced down at her stained and sweaty gown and immediately began to undress. She took her time in cleaning her skin with a cloth and bowl of water. Then she brushed out her long hair until it glistened before she put on a clean gown.

Anticipation of possibly seeing Ronan urged her down the stairs well before the evening meal. But once more, she was disappointed, as he was nowhere in sight.

With nothing else to do, Meg walked into the kitchens to help.

~ ~ ~

Ronan smiled when he saw the saffron shirt laid out on the bed along with another kilt. The Galt tartan was all he had ever worn, but it was filthy. He was no longer in a world he knew. Two centuries had passed, and much had changed in Scotland. Perhaps it was time he did as well.

The only claim he had to the Galt clan was his name, and even that didn't give him the desire to search them out. He had no coin, no home...nothing. He was well and truly on his own. There might have been something to interest him away from Ravensclyde if Stefan, Daman, and Morcant were with him.

Alone, well, that was a completely different story.

Meg had offered for him to remain at Ravensclyde for as long as he wanted. Oddly enough, he didn't feel the desire to leave. Was it

Meg holding him? Surely not. He knew better than to let a woman close.

It had to be the fact that he was alone. That was a solid explanation, and the only one he would even consider. Despite the fact his cock was already hardening at the mere thought of Meg.

Ronan removed his kilt and folded the tartan carefully before setting it atop the chest against the wall. He then pulled the saffron shirt over his head and let it settle against his skin. Next, he picked up the Alpin kilt and made quick work of putting it on.

He paused before leaving the chamber to run his fingers through his hair. It wasn't until he scratched his jaw that he felt the whiskers. It had been so long since he had to shave that Ronan had forgotten about it.

It was obvious someone else had thought of it though when he turned and found everything he needed to shave set on a small table near the window.

With a chuckle, Ronan set to work. It took longer than usual as he got used to holding the blade in his hand once more. At least he didn't cut his face. When he finished, he ran a hand over his jaw pleased not to feel any stubble.

He hurried out of the chamber, and only belatedly realized halfway down the stairs that it was excitement that urged him onward — excitement at seeing Meg again.

He came to a halt in the great hall when his eyes landed on her. She was a vision with her auburn locks flowing around her, the color like a beacon for him. She was talking to the servants when she glanced up and saw him. A soft, welcoming smile tilted her full lips as she stopped mid-sentence.

Ronan started toward her. With a quick word to the servants, Meg met him in the middle of the great hall. She eyed the kilt and gave a nod of approval.

"You look very handsome."

He gave her a wink. "It was a nice way of telling me my kilt needed to be cleaned."

"The Alpin kilt looks good on you."

She gestured to the table. "It's time for our meal."

They had no sooner taken their seats than the hall began to fill with people. Food was then brought out and set on the tables. Ronan looked around the great hall noting the ease in which everyone ate.

There had been too much tension between his parents and his uncle and aunt for there to have been a nice supper – or any meal for that matter.

"What did you do today?" Meg asked.

Ronan swallowed his bite and shrugged. "I began to fix a roof."

Meg paused in her eating to look at him. "You went back to the cottage."

He wasn't sure if she was happy or not since no emotion showed on her face. Ronan gave a small nod. "I want to earn my keep."

"And the discussion with the stable master?"

"He offered two of his sons to help me tomorrow."

For long moments, she silently stared at him. "Thank you. I've been trying to find the time to help the family, but there are few men to spare."

"That's what I'm for," he said, suddenly happy at the delight in her gray eyes.

"You would've been a good laird, Ronan."

He looked away. "It was never my position to have."

"Aye, but it's in your blood."

Ronan wanted to change the subject. He hated thinking of his past. "And how long will you be here?"

"Who knows," she replied flippantly.

But Ronan instantly knew she was keeping something from him. "I thought you said your aunt gave you leave to remain here."

"She did."

He took a drink of his ale and surveyed the great hall before he turned his head to her. "What are you no' telling me, lass?"

"Nothing," she was quick to assure him.

Ronan let it go. For the moment. It was difficult for him to concentrate with his body aching with desire for her. She was sitting next to him, but he couldn't touch her.

In all his years, not once had he held back from taking whatever he wanted. Why was he stopping now? Especially after already having Meg.

And the answer was the woman herself.

He wanted to protect her, shelter her. He saw the honesty and passion in her eyes. She looked at him as if he were worthy of her, and he found he desperately wanted to be worthy.

When the meal was finished, Ronan relaxed for a while before he scooted back his chair and held out his hand. "Walk with me, sweet Meg."

Her gray eyes darkened from the shared attraction and intimacy. How he wanted to jerk her against him and kiss her in front of everyone. To claim what was his.

With her hand in his, Ronan escorted her up the stairs to the battlements and out into the night.

"There are too many clouds to see the stars," Meg said.

"I didna bring you out here to see the stars. I brought you out here for this," he said as he pulled her against him and covered her mouth with his.

The explosion of desire was instantaneous, urgent.

Blazing.

His hands slid into the cool locks of her hair and held her captive as he ravaged her mouth. She was beauty, innocence, temptation, and strength.

She was his weakness, and his power.

His.

Ronan ended the kiss, his breathing harsh as he tried to control his raging body. Meg rested her head on his chest as they held each other.

"This is like a dream," she whispered into the night.

A dream that was unsettling. Ronan didn't understand the fierce feelings rolling through him. Maybe if he did he could just accept them.

It wasn't just the strange emotions, there was

also the burning need to claim her again that pounded through his veins with a constant beat.

He smoothed her hair away from her face and rested his chin atop her head. "If you doona talk of something, I'm going to lift your skirts right here and take you."

"That sounds...exciting."

Ronan closed his eyes and groaned. "Doona tempt me."

"What do I talk about?"

"You can tell me what you didna in the great hall. How long do you plan to remain at the castle?"

He felt her take a deep breath before she said, "Until Aunt Tilly dies, I suspect."

"Is she that aged?"

"She's an old woman. Many are surprised she has lived this long."

"And the castle is hers?"

"In a manner," Meg answered. "It was her brother's who had no heirs. He left the castle and lands to Aunt Tilly's eldest who is laird of his own castle."

Now Ronan understand it all. "You think your cousin will make you leave?"

"I'm sure he will."

"Why? You're taking care of his castle. I see it as a reason for him to want to keep you. If he doesna, he'll have to hire a steward to do it."

Meg's head lifted as she looked at him. "I hadn't thought of that. Do you really think he would consider it?"

"I doona see why you can no' plead your case if you do a good enough job, which it seems you have. Who was here before?"

"Aunt Tilly for several years, but she's taken to visiting family now. Until I came, there was no one."

Ronan chuckled. "It almost sounds like destiny."

"Almost."

Their gazes locked, and the simmering passion flared again. Ronan turned her toward the door to walk her to his chamber when a lone shape in the darkness snared his gaze.

Even from the distance he recognized the gypsy woman from the cottage, and a ripple of unease rippled down his spine.

CHAPTER SEVEN

Meg knew something was wrong by the way Ronan's body stiffened. She glanced over and spotted Ina just before the old woman moved back into the shadows.

"That was odd," Meg said as they entered the castle. "I can't remember the last time Ina left her cottage."

Ronan said not a word as he escorted her down the corridor. A glance at him showed Meg that anger and worry simmered just below the surface.

"She won't bother you," Meg told him.

"There will be little you can do to stop the gypsy."

"How do you know she's a gypsy? No one has ever said anything like that about Ina." Especially Aunt Tilly. In a short order of time, Meg had begun to think there really was something like magic in Scotland. And someone had to be able to use that magic.

"I know what she is," Ronan stated coldly. "It's in her eyes, and the way she stared at me. A gypsy recognizes one who has been cursed."

Meg stopped and faced Ronan, forcing him to halt as well. "You earned your freedom."

"Have I? I'm no' so sure. Knowing Ilinca, it wouldna be so easy as to find a woman who said I didna have to return to the mirror. Ilinca would make things much more difficult."

"What could you possibly do to ensure that the mirror would never be your prison again?" The thought of Ronan disappearing left her...cold.

"That wisdom she didna impart, and I suspect on purpose."

Meg might not be in control of her own life, but she could help Ronan. She covered her mouth as she faked a huge yawn. "It's been a long day."

"Aye," he said and frowned at her. "Let me see you to your chamber."

How deeply his mind was entranced with the curse was evident by the way he deposited her at her chamber door with a quiet good-night and turned on his heel to walk in the direction of his chamber.

Meg let out a long sigh. Magic. Gypsies. Mirrors as prisons. It was all laughable, or should be.

If Ina really were a gypsy, then she would be able to answer Meg's questions. Meg hurried down the stairs into the great hall and came to a halt when she saw Aunt Tilly standing in the doorway.

Aunt Tilly was a loud, boisterous sort that even old age couldn't dim. She was laughing at something one of the maids said, her voice easily carrying around the hall while she leaned heavily upon her cane.

Meg smiled as soon as Tilly's direct blue gaze landed on her. Her aunt opened her arms, and Meg walked into them to be enveloped in a fierce hug that was unexpected from the thin, frail looking woman.

"You look more yourself," Aunt Tilly said and then pulled back. She scrutinized Meg's face with shrewd eyes for several silent moments. "Meg, if I didn't know better, I'd say you found yourself a man."

Meg could feel the color drain from her face. No one was supposed to know. How had her aunt figured it out?

"About time," Aunt Tilly said and pulled her in for another hug.

Once released, Meg turned so that Tilly could lean on her as they walked to the solar. "I had no idea you were coming."

"I didn't either, my dear. Just a feeling I had that I wanted to see you. It seems your time at Ravensclyde has done you good."

"Very much so." Meg thought of Ronan and how he had touched her so gently.

"And the man?"

Meg swallowed, unsure of how much to tell Tilly. "He arrived recently and needed work. He's helping with odd jobs."

Aunt Tilly made an odd sound at the back of her throat. "And the furniture in the attic. Did you find anything that appealed to you?"

"Several pieces." She helped Tilly into a chair and sat beside her. "Some are being refinished or recovered. A few have already been dispersed throughout the castle after a good cleaning."

"That's good to hear, but was there anything in there that drew you?"

Maybe it was the way that Tilly's sharp blue eyes watched her so carefully, or maybe it was the tone her aunt used, but Meg had a feeling Aunt Tilly knew all about the mirror in the attic.

Her aunt suddenly smiled and sat back, both of her hands resting atop her cane. "Ah. I see that you found it. I suspect that your new worker is Ronan."

"You know him?" Meg felt as if the chair had been yanked from beneath her as the world tilted precariously.

"I do. He's the one who put that glow in your cheeks, isn't he?"

Meg nodded woodenly, still trying to grasp what was going on. "If you know Ronan, then you let him out of the mirror?"

"That was me, aye. Newly married into the Alpin family, I just happened to find the mirror that had been hidden in the attic."

"You put him back in that prison. Why?" Meg couldn't believe her aunt could be so cruel.

Aunt Tilly glanced at the floor. "I didn't want to, but Ina said I must."

"Ina. I was on my way to see her when you arrived."

"She wouldn't tell you anything, Meg. You see, she told me to put Ronan back in his prison until it was time for him to be released again."

Meg stood, appalled and angry. "So Ina is a gypsy? Do all gypsies hate Ronan so much that they want him to suffer for eternity? Ilinca said he could earn his freedom. I've given it to him."

"It's not that simple," Tilly said softly. She let out a long sigh, her stare hard and unmoving. "Sit, Meg. Please."

She wanted to rush up to Ronan, or out to Ina, and demand to know the truth. Instead, Meg resumed her seat and waited.

Tilly rubbed her swollen knuckles. "Aye, Ina is a gypsy. As I'm sure you've figured out, there is such a thing as magic in our wonderful land. The gypsies have a way with curses that make them so unbreakable that not even another gypsy can destroy it.

"Ina knew of the mirror. Her family had remained on Alpin land to keep watch over the times Ronan was let out."

Meg's shoulders slumped. "The first time he was released from the mirror he ran away. It was a gypsy that sent him back wasn't it?"

Tilly's face scrunched. "In a way. It was also his prison that pulled him back. I wanted to help Ronan."

"Then why didn't you?"

"Ina said there would be another Alpin woman

who would release him. There was a chance that he could earn his freedom at that time."

Meg licked her lips. "How does he earn his freedom?"

"Ina wouldn't tell me. Nor will she tell you," Tilly quickly said when Meg started to rise.

Meg huffed out a breath as she stayed seated. "I want to help him. He made a mistake, but he didn't kill Ana. She killed herself because she couldn't take rejection. Why should he be punished for that?"

Tilly reached over and set her gnarled hand atop Meg's. "Not everyone is as strong as you, my dear. Even in your darkest hour after that bastard ran off with your dowry and left you waiting at the altar, I knew you would come through it all."

"My chances at finding another man to marry are nonexistent, aunt. I have no dowry."

"For some, you won't have to."

Meg looked up at the ceiling as she once more thought of Ronan. "Wishful thinking on both our parts." Meg hated the pain she felt in her heart as she realized the truth of her words. "Ronan abhors marriage, and he has every right to after what his mother did to his father. He doesn't trust women."

"Do you...care...for him?"

Meg met her aunt's gaze. "I didn't think I'd ever be able to have feelings like this again. Ronan barreled into my life, but he has opened my heart and my mind to the possibility that happiness could be mine. If I dared to reach for it."

"Are you willing to fight for him?"

"Fight for a man that will do anything to keep from being married?" Meg asked in disbelief. The answer swelled within her. "If there is even a wee chance I could have a future with Ronan, I would have to do it honestly. No manipulation, no lies, and no deceit. I would have to win him with my feelings."

Tilly nodded in approval. "If anyone can do it, you can. You keep saying you care for him, and that you have feelings, but is it love?"

Was it love? Meg recalled how he had taken her in his arms and kissed her with such abandon, touched her with unrestraint.

Made love to her as if there were no tomorrow.

Her stomach quivered as she recalled the hungry desire that had flared in his eyes right before he kissed her. He hadn't spent all his time with her, and the women of the castle had certainly taken notice of him. Yet he hadn't eased himself with any of them. Only her.

Was it because she held the key to whether he returned to the mirror or not? The euphoria blossoming within her withered at the thought.

"Meg?" Aunt Tilly called.

Meg rose to her feet, her stomach a ball of knots. "I've had a very long day."

"Of course," her aunt said with sharp eyes. "Why don't you send Ronan down to me?"

Meg nodded as she hurried out of the solar and ascended the stairs. Each step weighted her down until she felt as if she carried the world upon her shoulders.

Her hand shook when she raised it to knock on Ronan's door. The door was yanked open, and Ronan stood before her, his eyes as troubled as before.

"You doona look well. Are you all right?" he asked.

Meg couldn't calm her heart it beat so fast. "Aunt Tilly just arrived. She would like to see you in the solar."

"All right. First, tell me what's wrong."

She hated the concern in his gaze. It made her feel special, and she knew better than most how easily she could be duped. She was afraid to ask Ronan why he was really with her, because she was terrified of the truth.

Meg tried to turn away, but Ronan pulled her against him, his strong arms wrapping around her. He held her to his chest, giving her comfort. "I doona know what I've done, but it wasna on purpose, whatever it is."

He was apologizing without knowing if he had even done anything. It would be so easy to love this man, to give him her whole heart and plan a life with him.

It all lay out before her, giving her a glimpse of what she could have.

Meg pulled out of his arms and met his gaze. "Thank you for today. I didn't think I could let a man that close again, but you proved me wrong. I'll have a good memory to wipe out the bad ones."

Ronan's heart missed a beat. Meg's speech sounded suspiciously like farewell. Her face was as pale as death, and her gray eyes filled with such sorrow that he searched his mind for a way to make it go away.

"What are you saying?" he asked.

"I'm saying you don't owe me anything for letting you out of the mirror. Don't feel obligated to woo me because you think I might get angry and send you back."

Ronan took a step back he was so shocked. It had never entered his mind that Meg would do that, which was more than odd since that's normally exactly how he would have approached her.

"That's no' what I was doing."

She backed away, a tight smile in place that didn't reach her eyes. "It's all right. I told you. I understand. My aunt is waiting for you."

Ronan stepped out of his chamber as Meg quickly walked away. He was so befuddled that he stared at her retreating back until she disappeared around a corner.

He had the unnerving feeling that Meg wanted nothing more to do with him. Anger replaced his bewilderment. There was only one person who could have turned Meg against him – Aunt Tilly.

CHAPTER EIGHT

Ronan couldn't hold back his fury as he rounded the corner and walked into the solar. Only to come to a halt as he recognized the blue eyes staring at him. They were older, but there was no mistaking the kindness he remembered so well.

"Matilda."

Tilly smiled. "Hello, Ronan. It's been many years since I last saw you. While you look the same, age has changed me."

He walked around Tilly taking in the cane, wrinkled skin, and white hair. "I didna think to ever see you again."

"I'm sure you would rather not have seen me again."

It was true. "You did put me back in."

"Ina said I must. She told me that you would be released again."

He sat, her words muddling his already puzzled mind. "You have no idea what it's like in that prison. There is only darkness."

"I know." Her voice was low, regret in every syllable. "I'm sorry, Ronan, and though you may not believe it, I did it to save you."

His mother's and sister's duplicitous actions filled his mind. They too were always remorseful when they were found out. It never lasted long though. "Is that right? Tell me how."

"Ina said there was a chance for you to gain your freedom for good."

This had him sitting up straighter. He held Tilly's gaze and leaned forward. "How?"

"That I don't know. Ina wouldn't tell me. I believe it's because she doesn't know herself."

"Then how can she know this might be my chance?" he yelled. Ronan stood and paced the solar, Tilly's words battering him like a fierce winter storm.

Everything within him urged him to go to Meg. It wasn't something he had ever done before. He didn't even know what to say to her. He only knew that he had to make right whatever had somehow gone wrong.

"Why did you turn Meg against me?" he asked with his back to Tilly. He couldn't stand to see the triumph in her gaze.

"I have no idea what you're talking about. I asked her if she cared for you. That's all it took to send her upstairs."

Ronan leaned his hands against the stone hearth and dropped his chin to his chest. "She said she was ill when she came here."

"Did she tell you why?"

"Aye."

There was a beat of silence before Tilly said, "That man broke her. Meg has always been such a trusting, accepting soul. There isn't a mean bone in her body, and yet the worst kind of man offered for her."

"Could you no' see him for what he was?"

"He fooled everyone. Including his own family, who have since disowned him. None of that can change what happened. Meg was given a hard lesson of life, and because of it, she'll spend the rest of her life here."

Ronan lifted his head and faced Tilly. "You're going to allow her to remain here?"

"I've already spoken to my son. His main concern is his clan, as it should be, but this is a holding of the Alpins. We don't want it to fall into the wrong hands."

"You need to let Meg know."

"That's part of the reason I'm here. The other part was to make sure she found your mirror."

Ronan ran a hand through his hair. "She thinks I'm beholden to her for releasing me. She thinks that's why I...spend my time with her."

"I know exactly what you two have done. I shouldn't condone it, but Meg needed what you've given her, Ronan. And I think you needed what she has given you."

He wasn't sure what to say, so he remained silent. While his imprisonment had changed him, it hadn't changed his view of women. Meg had done that all on her own. She had also wormed her way into his soul, embedding herself there so that no other woman would ever compare.

"You told Meg of your view on women. I know I factored into that as well, because I told you that I would keep you free, and then sent you back. Do you view Meg in the same light as other women?" Tilly asked.

"Never. Meg is...different. She could have done a great many things to get me to do whatever it was she wanted in return for staying out of the mirror. But she didna."

"Are you beholden to her?"

"She let me out. Fed me, conversed with me, and told me she would never send me back. Of course I'm beholden to her. Just no' in the way she thinks."

Tilly's astute blue eyes narrowed on him. "And you taking her innocence? Was that your way of thanking her?"

If he answered honestly, Ronan could very well find himself back in the mirror because he was talking to Meg's aunt. Yet there was no other choice.

"Part of my punishment from Ilinca was a constant, aching need that only another's touch could relieve. When I fell out of that mirror I wanted three things. The sun, a goblet of ale, and a woman. And no' necessarily in that order."

"So you used my niece?"

"I wanted her, aye. It was a yearning clawing at me, persistent and ever present. Her easy smile, her guileless gray eyes, and her sweet voice. That first night I went looking to ease myself on a willing woman. I found one, but I couldna go through with it. I kept thinking of Meg. What happened between us wasn't planned. I might have wanted her, but I wasn't going to use Meg in that way."

Tilly's white head cocked to the side. "Interesting. Would you say you care about her?"

Panic set in. Was Tilly cornering him into marriage? As much as he didn't want to hurt Meg, he wouldn't be forced. "I care about my freedom."

"I'm not talking marriage," Tilly said angrily. "I'm merely asking if you care about my niece. Even if I wanted you two together, that's not my decision to make."

Ronan swallowed. Did he care about Meg? Caring meant the woman had some measure of control over him. He refused to turn out like his father.

Even as he opened his mouth to say no, he remembered his last conversation with Meg. She had cried no tears, nor had she tried to wring any promises from him. She had simply walked away.

The feeling was...crushing. He wanted to go to her and shake her. Just before he kissed her.

"I know that look," Tilly said with a slight smile that would normally have set him on edge. "You do care for her, but you don't want to admit it.

She's ready to give you up, Ronan. Are you ready to let her go?"

"Nay."

The word burst from him. He wasn't done with Meg – wasn't done kissing her, touching her...knowing her.

By the saints, how had he come to this? How had he fallen for an auburn haired beauty without even knowing it? More importantly, what did he do about it?

"Have you ever loved, Ronan?"

He looked at Tilly and frowned. "My three friends. I loved them like brothers."

"Then you know what it means to care that deeply for someone. Is it enough, though?"

"Enough for what?"

"To win Meg. She won't settle for anything other than all of you."

Ronan knew that meant marriage. He had been so adverse to it for so long that he wasn't sure he could go through with it.

"I had a long, happy marriage," Tilly said. "Oh, we fought. Everyone has their spats, but there's nothing better than a long night of making up."

He smiled in spite of himself. "You could be lying."

"I could be. Look around, Ronan. You've been at Ravensclyde for a month. You've seen unhappy people as well as happy ones. That is life. It's up to each individual to make the most out of what they have. You," she said as she climbed to her feet with the help of her cane, "have a second chance. So does Meg. The two of you better not muck things up."

She slowly walked to the doorway before she turned to him. "Because if you do, you'll be back in the mirror, and she'll have a very lonely life."

CHAPTER NINE

Meg sat atop her bed without any candles lit and listened to the sounds of the castle. She had never minded the dark. It shielded her from prying eyes and hid the worst of her tears. She might welcome the darkness, but Ronan didn't.

She couldn't stop thinking of him, no matter how much she tried. Now, in the dark, she wondered how he had survived two hundred years trapped in the mirror without going daft.

He hadn't aged, hungered for food, or needed water. Whatever magic used must have made sure he wouldn't go insane either.

She let her mind wander over conversations she had with Ronan throughout the month. He was always quick with a smile and his charm. More often than not he made her laugh.

Little by little, he had become a constant in her life until she found herself wanting him with her. That want had somehow, inexplicably become need. He had shown her true desire. She recalled the story of his mother, and how he was cursed into the mirror.

Always it came back to that damn mirror. Without it she would never had met Ronan, and as long as the threat of him having to return to it hung over his head, she would never know if he was with her because he really wanted to be.

When the castle grew quiet, Meg rose and silently made her way out of her chamber to the stairs that led to the attic. She walked to the back room that held the mirror.

It stood as tall as a pillar and as eerie as an abyss. And yet Meg walked right up to it. She looked into the glass, but nothing of the room behind her was reflected.

She lifted her hand to the glass, ready to touch it, when she was suddenly spun away. Meg looked up into green eyes she had come to know so well.

"Doona test it," he whispered.

"The curse wasn't for me."

"It's no' something I want to prove. What are you doing up here?"

She shrugged, much too comfortable in his arms. When she tried to move out of his hold, he tightened his arms, preventing her. "When I can't sleep, I walk around the castle. What are you doing up here?"

"I came to see something."

"Did you find what you were looking for?"

"I'm no' sure yet."

Meg flattened her palms on his chest. "I better return to my chamber."

"Wait," he said hurriedly, almost nervously. "Just a few moments more."

She hesitated before she gave him a nod. This was a side of Ronan she hadn't seen before, and it intrigued her.

"Meg," he said, and then cleared his throat. "Have you spoken to your aunt again?"

"Nay."

"I'm sure she'll tell you in the morn, but your cousin is going to allow you to remain at Ravensclyde indefinitely."

Meg blinked at him. She didn't have to leave? She could call Ravensclyde her home? It seemed too good to be true. "Are you sure?"

"It's part of the reason your aunt came to visit."

Meg dropped her head against his chest, and felt as if a huge load had been taken off her shoulders. "I won't have to go to a convent or worry about finding relatives to allow me to stay with them."

"You get to make your own destiny. Including taking a husband."

She stiffened and slowly raised her head. If she could find a man who would take her without a dowry, then yes, there was a chance. But none of them would be Ronan. He had ruined her for any other man.

No one could give her that mischievous, wicked

smile like he did. No one could make her toes curl with a single kiss like he did. No one could make her heart race uncontrollably just by being near her as he did.

"I don't think so." Was that dejection she saw on his face? Surely not.

"I see."

She frowned, wondering at the odd tone in his voice. "What about you? Will you leave the castle now?"

"I couldna even if I wanted to."

Meg ignored the little thrill that shot through her. "What do you mean? It's the mirror, isn't it?"

Ronan wouldn't tell her that it had been pulling at him for a week now. He had been ignoring it, but then he found himself in the attic that night. Imagine his surprise when Meg walked right up to it.

Fear knifed through him, and he had reacted instantly in pulling her away. Even now, looking at the hated mirror, he wouldn't chance Meg being drawn in.

How much longer did he have before the mirror had him again? A day? An hour? Less?

He didn't want to go back into that dark prison without at least letting Meg know that she had changed his life. If only he had realized the chance he had and not ignored the feelings that had been growing.

But it was too late for him and Meg now. She no longer trusted him.

"I'm staying because I want to. I'm staying

because of you, because I...love you, sweet Meg."

Ronan didn't know what he thought would happen, but her silence was deafening. It was what he deserved. He had been going through the past weeks as if his life was his to control once more.

All those wasted hours he could have been wooing Meg to love him. They had been glorious days, and he was thankful they would get him through more centuries in the darkness until – if – anyone ever released him from his prison again.

Knowing he loved Meg and she didn't return his feelings was painful. It must have been what Ana experienced, and why she took her own life.

"You love me?" Meg asked in a soft voice.

Ronan couldn't stop touching her. His hands reverently cupped her face. "I didna realize it until tonight when you were putting a wall between us. I had to let you know before..."

"Before what?" she pressed.

He smiled, his heart breaking inside his chest. "My time here is up, sweet Meg."

Her gaze darted to the mirror. "I said you could remain. I'm not sending you back."

"I know. It's the curse. When I'm released, I guess I go through a test of sorts." At least now he knew what he needed to earn his freedom – love.

He could have had that with Meg, he knew it in the depths of his soul. If only he had realized what he would need to fight for. But it was too little, too late.

"You can't leave," she said, her voice becoming shrill. "I'm not ready for you to leave."

"Neither am I."

Ronan tried to tell her he loved her again when the edges of his vision went black. He could hear Meg screaming his name, but it sounded far away, and growing fainter by the moment.

He blinked, and the next instant he was back in the mirror. The desolation was severe, the despair intense.

The anguish fierce.

His sweet Meg was gone from him forever. He threw back his head and bellowed, putting every ounce of regret into it.

Meg slammed her hands against the mirror, the inky glass unswayed by her attack. She hollered for Ronan again and again, but he didn't answer.

She refused to let him go, even as the fear for the love growing inside her overwhelmed her. Meg sank to her knees, her hands sliding down the mirror as the tears came.

"Ronan. I love you, too."

Suddenly Meg was thrown backwards as a blinding white light erupted from the mirror. Something was tossed out before the light disappeared again.

Meg looked over to find Ronan on his side unmoving. She hastily crawled to him and rolled him onto his back. "Ronan," she called as she touched his face and smoothed back his hair. "Ronan, open your eyes and look at me."

A relieved laugh erupted from her when his lids opened to pin her with his green gaze. "Did you say-"

"Aye. I love you," she interrupted him as she dashed away tears. "I'm terrified of what will happen now, but I couldn't deny the truth, especially when you were back in the mirror."

He pulled her down atop him and kissed her deeply, passionately. Ronan then rolled them over until he leaned over her.

"I doona want to waste another moment. Stand by me for eternity, Meg. Be my wife."

"I'd love nothing better."

EPILOGUE

Two weeks later...

Ronan couldn't believe he was actually getting married. The fortnight had seemed an eternity as he waited impatiently to make Meg his own.

Tilly had remained at Ravensclyde getting everything in order for the wedding. The entire castle had come out for the event.

Ronan looked around the bailey at all the smiling faces, including Tilly's son Angus and his wife. Angus had pulled him aside and offered Ravensclyde as his and Meg's home as long as they held it for him.

He had found a home at Ravensclyde, a life that seemed brighter than he could have ever hoped. The only thing missing were his friends. Ronan would do anything if he could have Daman,

Morcant, and Stefan standing with him.

It was a bittersweet moment missing his friends so terribly while being so happy. The melancholy, however, diminished when he caught sight of Meg standing on the steps of the castle.

She looked enchanting in a gown of deep green. Her auburn locks flowed freely down her back with a simple circle of white and yellow flowers around her head.

Her smile was wide as she made her way to him. Ronan took her hand as soon as she was near. He feared she might run away or change her mind about marrying him if he didn't.

"I'm yours," she whispered with a wink.

Ronan felt the grip on his heart ease. They faced the priest as the ceremony began. Ronan couldn't believe magic had taken him from his home into a prison, but it had also delivered him to Meg.

More magic had happened when love blossomed, and now he was going to have her for the rest of his life.

Applause erupted as the ceremony ended, and Meg faced him once more.

"You're officially mine," he told her. "You willna get away from me now."

"You have me forever."

"That willna be long enough," he whispered before he sealed their vows with a kiss.

Look for the next Rogues of Scotland story
THE HUNGER
September 2014!

Until then, read on for a peek at
DARKEST FLAME
the first full length book in the New York
Times bestselling series Dark Kings arriving
April 29, 2014

Kellan kept utterly still in his corner. The sound of water sloshing against stone woke him instantly. He opened one eye to see the normally glass-like surface rippling violently as he caught sight of a human emerging from the water.

He barely had time to register it was a heavily breathing woman before a second joined her—this one male.

Kellan shifted his head to get a better look. It had been many centuries since he'd seen a human, and quite frankly, he could go through eternity without seeing another. How he despised them.

He didn't like his sleep being disturbed either. Yet, he knew Constantine wouldn't be happy if he made himself known in his dragon form and ate the two intruders . . . as tempting as that might be.

His only other option would be to shift into human form and confront them. And that was too distasteful to even consider.

Kellan stayed in his spot and watched as the two

circled each other. *Nothing's changed. Humans are always fighting.*

No matter how many centuries passed, no matter what country he visited, they were all the same. Selfish, belligerent, arrogant, greedy bastards.

Not that he cared how many humans killed each other. The more dead meant they were that much closer to the dragons returning home. It was because of the humans that dragons no longer ruled the realm.

It was humans who had begun the war.

But it had been dragons who ended it.

The humans were talking. Kellan listened to their exchange with interest. He thought back to the many times Con had visited him while he slept, and realized it had been many, many, *many* centuries since he last woke.

Con's visits every few decades kept those dragons who wished to sleep away centuries—or millennia—up to date on the world so when they awoke they were more or less knowledgeable about the times. So it wasn't difficult for Kellan to make out what the humans were saying.

The male disliked the female according to the way disdain dripped from his voice. Surprisingly, the female didn't cower. She fought back, moving quickly—for a mortal—and striking the male deftly and accurately. None of her punches or kicks went astray.

Kellan smelled blood. It had been a long time since that scent assaulted him. It made him think of the last time he had walked among humans—and why he had chosen to sleep.

There was a grunt from the pair. The male had a broken nose and a cut lip, but the scent Kellan held was strong, too strong for such paltry wounds.

His dragon eyes locked on the female, and he caught sight of her left arm held protectively against her side. Blood ran thick and fast down her leg to drip upon the stones.

In a whirl, the female came up with a weapon of her own.

Kellan's interest sharpened when the male said he wanted to wound the female. It wasn't hard to guess she was to lure the dragons.

He inwardly snorted. Stupid humans. They all thought dragons base creatures who wanted to eat everything in sight or char it. How could he and the other Dragon Kings have fallen so far?

They used to rule the skies, the seas, and the earth. Every dragon of every color had called earth home. They had reigned supreme.

And for Kellan and the other Dragon Kings, it had been their right to rule their dragons, keeping everyone in line. That's not to say there weren't battles, but with one word from a Dragon King, all fighting would cease.

How Kellan longed for the days of old. He missed his dragons, and he missed being able to take to the skies whenever he wanted. It's one of the many reasons he decided to sleep away the time. He couldn't look upon the earth and humans without wanting to kill them all.

Kellan was impressed with the female, even though he hated to admit it. She was a valiant fighter, and though she was wounded, she was winning.

She moved in a lightning-quick spin before she kicked her opponent to the ground. Then she landed on top of him and sunk her blade into his heart.

Just like that, the battle was over.

The female had lost too much blood, however. She

couldn't swim back out, and she didn't know her way through the caves of the mountain to seek help.

The only one that could help her was Kellan. And that wasn't going to happen. There would be hell to pay with Con, but Kellan had ceased to care long ago.

He wouldn't return to sleep until she had breathed her last though. Kellan expected her to fall over and die, or try to find her way out.

Instead, she kicked the male away and leaned back against a boulder before pulling some sticks from a pocket on the leg of her skin-tight suit. She bent them, and with a slight *pop,* green light shone around her.

She set those aside and took another small pack from a pocket next to her ankle on her other leg. Her breathing was harsh, and sweat coated her skin.

"Shit," she murmured and swallowed audibly.

Her accent wasn't Scots or British. Kellan went through all the dialects Con had played for him over the centuries in his mind until he reached American.

Could that be why the Brit hadn't cared for her? It was a silly reason, but then again, humans rarely made sense.

Kellan forgot about accents as the female reached behind her and grabbed something. There was a zipping noise before her black suit loosened.

With a grunt she pulled her right arm out of the black material before carefully extracting her left. She pushed the thick fabric down, giving Kellan a view of a small top that held her breasts. A bathing suit, he recalled.

Her chest heaved as she tried to breathe through the pain and her skin grew pale. Once more she took the small black parcel she pulled from the pocket of her leg and opened it. She grabbed a white packet and tore it open using her teeth. She briefly closed her eyes before pouring the tiny granules over her wound.

A gasp passed her lips as she jerked from the contact. Kellan had never had much to say about humans, but he had to give the female credit. Her hands were coated with blood, her arms shook, she was weak, and it was dark, yet she never gave up.

His interest was piqued when he saw her pull out a curved needle and thread. With her wound on her left side, she had to twist to see it, yet she managed to get several stitches done before she slowly fell unconscious.

For long minutes, Kellan stared at her. The female was slumped to her side, her breathing low and irregular. He knew that a fever could soon overtake her.

If it were up to him, he would forget her. She'd die—as all mortals did. Then Kellan remembered why he had chosen to sleep. He had made a vow once, a promise he had broken because of his hatred of humans.

Con could have ended his life, but he had allowed Kellan his sleep. He seriously doubted Con would give him another pass. Constantine was the King of Dragon Kings. He was the ultimate law—though that never stopped any other Dragon King from doing what he had to do.

Con took their duty of protecting humans seriously. If it had been up to Kellan, he'd have wiped the world of mortals long ago. They were an infection that stained everything. Look what they had done to dragons.

Everything known about dragons was nothing more than a myth, feared and fantasized into something that wasn't even close to resembling what life as a dragon really was.

Kellan vividly remembered standing after a battle

with the humans to find his beloved Bronzes littered upon the ground. The bronze dragons were the Bringers of Justice.

While Kellan had ordered them to protect the humans, the humans had in turn killed them. A betrayal that even now, thousands of millennia later, Kellan couldn't forgive.

Because even though dragons were supposed to defend mankind, mankind had never wanted their protection. The mortals had sought early on to betray the very beings that had ruled the land first.

But Kellan hadn't been the only one betrayed. Ulrik, King of Silvers, had been deceived by a human female—and then by the rest of the Dragon Kings.

Kellan squeezed his eyes closed as he thought of that day. If he'd known what would become of his Bronzes, he'd have sided with Ulrik.

In the end, the dragons had been the ones to lose everything. Con had sent them to another realm.

And the Kings remained behind.

What good were they though? The few times Kellan woke from his sleep and faced the world, he found his brethren hidden away in plain sight, waiting until cover of darkness or a storm to dare to take to the skies.

Flying was their right, their privilege, and even that had been taken away. Because of humans.

Hours ticked by while he mused over his hatred of man, but still the female didn't so much as twitch. Kellan would have no choice but to bring her to Con, because he didn't trust himself to try and see to her wound.

Hatred didn't so easily dissipate through the centuries.

He wasn't ready to wake from his sleep, but with

the two humans invading his mountain, Con would want to investigate. Kellan also found himself curious at the intrusion.

Using the telepathic ability between all Dragon Kings, Kellan called out Con's name, knowing his friend would arrive quickly. With barely a thought, Kellan shifted into human form. He rotated his arms and shook out his legs. There were no clothes for him to don because he'd had no intention of waking for many more millennia.

He walked naked to the woman and squatted beside her. Kellan didn't have the power to heal her as Con did. The bleeding had slowed, but it hadn't stopped.

Kellan shifted the woman onto her back, noting how hot her skin was to the touch. His body, however, responded instantly to the softness of the female, and it infuriated him. His body needed release, but it wouldn't be by this woman.

Promptly ignoring his thickening cock and the soft curves of the female's breast, Kellan picked up the needle she had been using and finished stitching the wound.

The male had managed to miss any of her vital organs, but the wound was long and deep. As delicate as humans were, Kellan knew Con was needed if she was to live. The choice of whether she died or not would be Con's.

Once Kellan finished, he bit the thread with his teeth and tied it off before lifting the woman into his arms. The feel of her curves reminded him of the yearning for a release clawing at him. He had to see to it. It wasn't because of this particular female in his arms. It had just been too long.

Kellan told himself that once more for good

measure before he strode from his cave.

Many of his fellow Dragon Kings had taken human females as lovers. Kellan had had several before his Bronzes were killed. Afterward, he took a female only when he could stand it no more.

It was unfortunate that his body demanded such release. He glanced down at the woman in his arms. She was thin, but her muscles were finely honed. Her dark hair was held back away from her face in a knot so he had no idea how long it was.

Kellan barely looked at her face. There was no need. He never planned to see her again once he deposited her at Con's feet, even though Kellan admired her courage and tenacity. That's all she would get from him.

That's all he could give.

It was much more than he had given a human in thousands of years.

Kellan navigated the corridors of his mountain easily until he came to the entrance. Just as he expected, Con, along with Rhys and Kiril, stood waiting for him.

Thank you for reading **THE CRAVING**. I hope you enjoyed it! If you liked this book – or any of my other releases – please consider rating the book at the online retailer of your choice. Your ratings and reviews help other readers find new favorites, and of course there is no better or more appreciated support for an author than word of mouth recommendations from happy readers. Thanks again for your interest in my books!

Donna Grant

www.DonnaGrant.com

ABOUT THE AUTHOR

New York Times and *USA Today* bestselling author Donna Grant has been praised for her "totally addictive" and "unique and sensual" stories. She's written more than thirty novels spanning multiple genres of romance including the bestselling Dark King stories, *Dark Craving*, *Night's Awakening*, and *Dawn's Desire*. Her acclaimed series, Dark Warriors, feature a thrilling combination of Druids, primeval gods, and immortal Highlanders who are dark, dangerous, and irresistible. She lives with her husband, two children, a dog, and four cats in Texas.

Find Donna Grant online at:

www.DonnaGrant.com

www.facebook.com/AuthorDonnaGrant

www.twitter.com/donna_grant

www.goodreads.com/donna_grant

Never miss a new book
From Donna Grant!

Sign up for Donna's email newsletter at
www.DonnaGrant.com

Be the first to get notified of new releases and be eligible for special subscribers-only exclusive content and giveaways. Sign up today!